Also by Denise Swanson

DEVEREAUX'S DIME STORE MYSTERIES

Fly Me to the Tomb

<u>A Devereaux's Dime Store Mystery</u>

Denise Swanson

http://www.DeniseSwanson.com

Fly Me to the Tomb

Copyright 2021 by Denise Swanson Stybr

Cover illustration created by Jaclyn Webber, Junco Portraits and Illustrations

ISBN-13: 978-0-9861017-7-9

Fly Me to the Tomb
A Devereaux's Dime Store Mystery
From *New York Times* best-selling author Denise Swanson.

When Aaron Burgess is found slumped over the steering wheel of his tractor and rushed to the Underwood Medical Clinic by his friend and business partner Quito Escobar, no one expected that the situation would turn into a homicide investigation. But when it does, newly licensed private investigator Devereaux Sinclair and her fiancé Jake Del Vecchio are hired to find the murderer. Was Aaron a random victim of some psycho killer or was his murder something much much more personal?

* * *

Love is in the air of Shadow Bend, Missouri. Dev and Jake are engaged and moving in together. Jake's ex-wife is working for and dating Dev's ex-boyfriend. And Jake's Uncle Tony has been reunited with his first sweetheart, Birdie. It even looks as if Dev's BFF, Boone St. Onge, has found his special someone.

But romance comes to a screeching halt when a mysterious murder takes place. This puzzle isn't just whodunnit, but how and why.

With a short list of suspects, Dev and Jake are in a race to figure out the answers before someone else gets planted six feet under.

CHAPTER 1
Devereaux

I backed up against the wall, making myself as small as possible in order to allow my fiancé, Jake Del Vecchio, to squeeze by carrying his load of boxes. Once he'd made it past me, he turned and winked before proceeding into what had once been my father Kern's childhood bedroom.

Even after Dad's marriage, his mother, Birdie, had kept it exactly as he left it. She might have preserved it as a tribute to his youth for sentimental reasons, but knowing my grandmother, it was more her way of expressing an opinion on the chances of his staying married.

Gran had not been a fan of my father's choice of wife, and although it had taken longer than she predicted, my parents had separated when I was sixteen. Right after Dad was sent to prison for a crime he didn't commit.

Always one to cut her losses, as soon as the verdict was in, Mom had promptly started divorce proceedings. Once those documents were finalized, she abandoned me at Birdie's and fled to parts unknown.

"Devereaux Ann Sinclair," Gran bellowed from the kitchen, snapping me out of my gloomy reflections, "you make sure that boy doesn't break any of Tony's records. Those albums are irreplaceable."

I rolled my eyes. First of all, my middle name was not Ann, and second of all, Jake was six foot four of well-muscled man. He was about as far from being a boy as I was from being a model.

Yeah. I was well aware that nowadays there were more curvy beauties walking the runways, but the fashion industry considered plus size to be between an eight and a twelve, which I definitely exceeded. I'm not saying by how much.

Oops! I must have been lost in thought for too long because Birdie appeared in the kitchen doorway with her hands on her hips and hollered down the hallway, "Did you hear me?"

Snickering, I shouted back, "Jake's carrying in Tony's clothes now. He already put the records in the living room next to the stereo."

Yes. Gran still had a stereo. It was a vintage Sears Roebuck Silvertone cabinet model that she had originally purchased in the sixties. Tony's vinyl albums would feel right at home on its turntable.

A smile relaxed Birdie's worry-sharpened features, and she said, "You two kids are so thoughtful." Wiping her hands on her apron, she added, "I bet you both could use a break, and lunch is almost ready, so go wash up."

Stepping away from the wall, I headed toward my room—at least it was mine for another hour or so. After that, I wouldn't be able to claim the bedroom that I had occupied for the past decade and a half.

This was the big day. Ever since I had admitted to myself that I was in love with Jake, we'd been discussing the logistics of getting married and moving in together.

We were both in our thirties and old enough to know what we wanted. We'd wasted enough time, him in a previous marriage and me on a thankless career, to realize that we didn't need to allow any amount of prescribed time to go by before making the decision to become husband and wife.

Our first obstacle had popped up six months ago while we were on our first romantic weekend as a couple. Jake's great-uncle Tony Del Vecchio had fallen and broken his hip.

Once Tony was better, Gran announced that she really, really wanted me to have the wedding ceremony in the Catholic Church. However, between my nonattendance and Jake's divorced status, her priest had refused to officiate.

Of course, my attempt at humor during that initial meeting with Father Flagg probably hadn't helped. I thought my comment that atheism was a non-prophet organization was funny. The priest did not.

Admitting defeat on the religious front, Gran starting pushing for an elaborate reception, which would take at least a year to plan. There just weren't that many venues in the area of our small rural community, and those were booked far, far in advance of the date.

Jake and I had compromised with Gran by agreeing to her vision of a fancy shindig if we could move in together while we waited for the big day to arrive. The question was how to accomplish that goal.

Before falling in love with Jake, I had made the commitment to stay with Gran in order to keep her out of assisted living. Her mild memory issues made it unwise for her to live alone, and she'd refused to let me hire someone to be with her.

Jake had made a similar vow to live with his great-uncle. Tony was no longer able to physically run the Del Vecchio cattle ranch, and Jake had agreed to become the official manager.

Between Tony's and Gran's age and their issues associated with being octogenarians, neither Jake nor I felt like we could leave them on their own. Even if it meant he and I couldn't live together until we figured out how to keep our loved ones safe without us with them.

One thing that had helped our search for a solution was that Birdie and Tony had dated when they were teenagers. The only reason they didn't end up married was that Tony was two years older than

Gran, and she had refused to drop out of school to become his wife.

While waiting for her to graduate, Tony enlisted in the marines. It was near the end of the Korean War, and when he turned up missing in action, Gran married someone else—my grandfather. Now that Birdie and Tony had both lost their spouses and reconnected, they were courting again.

The obvious answer was for Tony to move in with Gran and for me to move in with Jake. As to which couple lived where, with Jake running the day-to-day cattle operations, having us at the ranch was the sensible choice. That left Tony and Gran at her house.

Unfortunately, Jake and I didn't think the elderly couple should be left without someone to help out. And neither of them was willing to have us employ a person in that capacity.

You would have thought that with my father finally released from prison and living in Gran's garage apartment, he could have kept an eye on the ageing Romeo and Juliet. Sadly, that would have been too easy.

Dad had recently fallen for Catherine, a local artist who owned a gallery in town. He was now spending more time at her place than at home. And after all those years when he was incarcerated despite his innocence, I wasn't about to ask him to sacrifice even a moment of his newfound happiness for mine.

Happily, Gran's desire for Jake and me to

produce great-grandchildren, even out of wedlock, overcame her need for independence. After a few months of brooding about the situation, she had grudgingly allowed us to hire her and Tony what we were calling a housekeeper.

That gave us the perfect opportunity to find someone who had elder care experience. He or she would live in my old room and help Gran and Tony in whatever way they needed.

We'd been extremely fortunate that when the local queen of Shadow Bend society, Nadine Underwood, went into assisted living, her caretaker, Beckham Janson had hung around the area taking short-term assignments. We'd counted our lucky stars that we'd been able to snap him up before he found anything permanent. It wasn't as if there were a surplus of home health aides available in our tiny Missouri town.

Even luckier, Beck liked cats. Because if he hadn't been able to tolerate Banshee, Gran's elderly Siamese, the whole deal would have been off.

In fact, I think the clincher with Gran was when Banshee actually allowed Beck to pet him. I'd lived with the finicky feline for nearly fifteen years and he'd never willingly let me touch him.

Beck had been happy to accept what was actually a pretty cushy job. He mostly just needed to be present and chauffeur them wherever they wanted to go. Gran would certainly continue to cook and clean, and Tony was getting around better and better every day.

He might even be able to drive his beloved truck again. That is, if he could pass the driver's test that he'd need to take before his upcoming birthday. He was a bit of terror behind the wheel, and Jake maintained that his uncle didn't have to adopt a highway because he already drove like he owned the road.

Thankfully my business, Devereaux's Dime Store and Gift Baskets, was doing well, and I could swing my half of Beck's salary and benefits. While Jake had enough money to pay the whole tab, my pride wouldn't let me accept that offer. I just had to hope that nothing went wrong with my fragile financial security until after we were married, when we'd pool our resources.

Once we were husband and wife, I wouldn't mind that he added more to our joint finances than me. After all, a part of his assets was a trust fund set up for him by his wealthy parents to assuage their guilt about sending him to a boarding school so they could continue their jet-setter lifestyles. It wasn't my fault that my family didn't have the capital to do that for me.

Besides, money wasn't everything. Jake and I had already made it over a lot of hurdles to be together, and tonight we would be sharing the new king-size bed that would be delivered to the ranch this afternoon.

With that happy thought in mind, I went in

search of my fiancé. Birdie had just yelled that lunch was ready, and I could smell her famous pot roast calling my name.

CHAPTER 2
Devereaux

"I thought Birdie would never let us go." Jake helped me from his truck, then stepped around me to grab the cartons and luggage from the back seat of the extended cab.

Once Jake had added running boards to his Ford F250, I really didn't need help getting into or out of the huge pickup anymore. But I think we both enjoyed the sensation as my body slid down his.

"Gran really wanted us to stay for supper." I felt a little guilty declining her offer to cook for us, but Jake and I had been waiting a long time to live in a house together as a couple, and we'd been planning our first meal after I officially moved in for at least a week. "I hope our refusal didn't hurt her feelings too much."

"Nah." Jake gave me the handle of my rolling suitcase and the Tupperware pie keeper. He then stacked the two remaining boxes, anchored them with his chin, and carried them up the sidewalk toward the ranch house. "Just before she presented you with that black walnut caramel tart and waved goodbye, I caught Tony whispering to Birdie about great-grandchildren and us needing to be alone."

"Ah." I nodded my understanding while avoiding the cracks in the cement as I followed him. "That explains why Gran nearly shoved us out the door. I thought that she was angry with me."

Jake strode up the steps, then juggled the cartons as he searched his pockets for his key ring. If it were me, I would have kept it in my hand after I took it from the pickup's ignition, but instead of sharing my organizational wisdom, which my fiancé probably wouldn't appreciate, I considered my new home.

Of course, I'd been to the Del Vecchio residence several times while Jake and I tried to figure out our living arrangements, but now that it was ours, I studied the place with a fresh eye. It was a lot larger and fancier than Gran's place, and for just a second, I felt insecurity trickle through my veins. What was I doing moving in somewhere that looked a lot like Tara?

Granted, the huge southern colonial had seen better days, but the imposing white columns and stately wraparound porch were still daunting to a girl who had grown up in a run-down farmhouse. Which made it hard not to make the comparison between Jake's upbringing and mine.

His father was a plastic surgeon; mine had only

recently gotten out of prison. His mother was a socialite; mine was a gold-digger. His great-uncle owned over two thousand acres and ran six hundred and fifty head of cattle; my grandmother had barely been able to make ends meet. In fact, right after Dad's incarceration, Birdie had had to sell what remained of our farmland to Tony in order to keep us off of welfare.

"I should carry you across the threshold," Jake said, interrupting my discouraging thoughts.

Noticing that he'd managed to get the door open, I quickly moved inside, then said, "After we're married."

"I didn't realize you were such a traditionalist." Jake nudged me out of his way and deposited the boxes on the floor in the foyer.

"Me either." I shook off my melancholy mood and looked around.

The curving staircase was gorgeous but showed the same signs of neglect as the exterior. Between his wife's death and his own deteriorating health, Tony had pretty much abandoned an attempt at upkeep for the house, and the ranch had suffered as well. That was one of the reasons Jake had left the U.S. Marshals service and taken over managing the operation.

Another motive had been the injury that he'd suffered in the line of duty. At first, it had looked as if he'd never walk again, which was when his wife had divorced him, but even when Jake had recovered, he knew he'd never be a hundred percent again.

The third reason was me. Our growing love for one another had tipped the scales toward Jake's early retirement.

Leaving law enforcement had not been easy for him, and I'd been thrilled when he'd announced he'd gotten his private detective license to keep his hand in the game. He'd handled a couple of tricky cases that the police had not wanted to touch, and bringing justice to people who might otherwise have never gotten satisfaction seemed to have made Jake's transition from marshal to rancher a lot easier.

I could only hope he truly was content with the arrangement. It certainly had made me happy.

Now, as we both stood, gazing at our new home, it was the first time that I fully understood the extent of what we had to tackle to bring this place back to its former glory. Or even a tiny degree of it.

Sadly, unless we dipped into Jake's trust fund, which, due to his feelings about his parents, he'd vowed only to use in an emergency, we wouldn't be able to afford to fully restore the place for a long, long time. Personally, I would have used their dough and still not forgiven them for their neglect, but Jake was made of more honorable stuff than I.

Most of my available money was earmarked for Gran's half of the healthcare aide, and Jake was using his disability pension from the marshal service for Tony's part. Which meant, until Jake increased the ranch's production or my store started earning more, we had to be careful what we spent on ourselves. Because Tony had let things slide on the ranch, there was a lot of maintenance that needed to be paid for out of whatever profits Jake got out of the place.

In the meantime, we'd taken over the master bedroom and bath on the ground floor. That, along with the office, family room, and kitchen, would be where we spent most of our time, and while they were in better shape than the rest of the house, they still needed a major cleaning and lots of TLC.

I was deciding which projects to attempt first when Jake nuzzled my neck and murmured, "I hope you're not regretting moving in here with me."

"Well," I drew out the word, "it is a little more dilapidated than I realized."

"But there are fringe benefits." He nibbled my ear.

"True." Shivers raced down my spine. "How about you show me those after I shower."

"Or we could shower together?" Jake kept kissing his way down until he hit my cleavage.

"Next time," I promised, heading into the kitchen to put down the tart that I was still holding. "At the moment, I feel too grungy to be in the proper mood for a romantic shower scene."

Checking the time, I saw that it was going on four in the afternoon. We didn't plan to have dinner until six. Gran had fed us a big lunch, and we wanted to have a good appetite for the filets that had come from the ranch's own cattle. Still, I wanted to get squared away and cleaned up before we started cooking.

Once I'd deposited our dessert on the counter, I rolled my suitcase into the master bedroom. This bag contained the last of the clothes that I had kept at Gran's.

The boxes that Jake had carried in held books and pictures that I would arrange on the shelves that bracketed the fireplace in the living room. For someone on the other side of thirty, I didn't really own much other than my store.

After I unpacked, I stripped off my jeans and sweatshirt and stepped into the shower. Thankfully, the master bath had been remodeled a few years before Jake's aunt had passed away, so that was one less renovation Jake and I had to do.

While I was washing my hair, I heard the faint music that indicated that I was getting a call on my cell phone. Too bad I had no idea where it was currently located.

A few minutes later, it sounded as if Jake's was getting a call too. The situation reminded me of the first time he and I had tried to spend a weekend in Kansas City. And not in a good way.

I hurriedly finished my shower, wrapped a towel around my wet curls, slipped into my terry-cloth robe, and went in search of my missing phone.

Locating my purse in the nightstand drawer—why I had put it there was a complete mystery—I dug through it until I found my cell. It indicated that I had one message.

When I quickly accessed my voicemail, a familiar voice said, "Dev, I hate to bother you, but I need you and Del Vecchio to come to my clinic ASAP. The whole town could be in danger if we don't figure this out."

I was still standing staring at the little black device in my hand when Jake appeared in the bedroom doorway and asked, "Was that Underwood?"

"Uh-huh, his message said—"

"Yep," Jake cut me off, "I just got off the phone with him. Throw on some clothes and meet me at the truck. There's no time to waste."

CHAPTER 3
Jake

Jake gazed across the bench seat of his F250. There was an adorable crease between Devereaux's eyebrows as she buckled her safety belt and flipped down the sun visor. He waited for her to get settled, then threw the pickup into gear and drove around the half-circle driveway in front of the house, exiting onto the long private road that led to the paved street.

Once he made that turn, it was a straight shot into Shadow Bend, and he glanced at Dev. He hadn't given her much time to dress, and she'd put on the first outfit she found—black yoga pants, a long-sleeve bluish-green T-shirt that matched her incredible eyes, and a pair of black sneakers.

Going out of the front door, he'd grabbed her leather jacket and slipped it over her shoulders. It might be April, but spring in northwestern Missouri was still cold.

Heck. It wasn't even unheard of for them to get

some more snow before it truly warmed up.

As Dev pulled her wet hair over her shoulder and started combing it, she asked, "Did Noah give you any details about the emergency?"

"Some guy brought his friend into Underwood's medical clinic." Jake was surprised it had taken her this long to ask. One of the things he loved about her was her keen curiosity and razor-sharp mind. "The guy was drenched in sweat, drooling, and could barely stand."

"That's awful." Dev dug through her purse, retrieved a hair tie, and fastened it around the end of the braid she'd just finished. "But I don't see how that could be something that endangered the whole town."

Jake eased up on the gas pedal. It wouldn't help anyone if he wrecked the truck or got pulled over for speeding. "Underwood determined that the guy had somehow been poisoned, but he can't figure out what kind of toxin it might be or how the stuff got into his system."

"Ah…" Dev trailed off, the mascara wand she'd been using hovering between the mirror and her eyelash. "Noah thinks it might be airborne or in the water."

"Or that someone is deliberately poisoning people," Jake added.

"Oh, my goodness!" She shook her head. "There could be a mass murderer at large."

"Exactly." Jake nodded.

At first, Jake had been suspicious of Underwood's

call. It hadn't been any secret around town that today was the day that he and Devereaux were moving in together, and the good doctor was her old high school boyfriend. Add the fact that Underwood had been trying to rekindle that flame for the past couple of years, and Jake suspected that this emergency was just another attempt to throw a monkey wrench into his relationship with Devereaux.

Devereaux continued to put on her makeup in silence, then a few seconds later asked, "Did Noah call Chief Kinkaid?"

"Yep. The chief told Underwood not to be so dramatic and hung up on him."

"Hmm." Devereaux used her pinky to smooth the peachy-colored gloss she'd just applied, and Jake nearly went in the ditch before he could tear his gaze from her luscious lips. "I wonder if Chief Kinkaid's attitude has anything to do with the fact that Underwood is going out with your ex."

Jake had brought Meg, his former wife, to Shadow Bend after she'd been brutally assaulted by a serial killer. She had also been a US Marshal, and actually she still was but was currently on leave.

Even after her physical wounds from that homicidal maniac had healed, Meg remained catatonic. Since she had no family, the doctors were about to put her in a long-term care facility when Jake had stepped in. It had almost cost him his relationship with Devereaux, but he just couldn't let his ex rot in a state-run institution.

Meg had finally recovered—faster than she let on—and decided to stick around. Still feeling unfit to resume her marshal duties, she'd taken a job at Underwood's clinic as the receptionist and ended up dating the good doctor.

Yep. Devereaux's old boyfriend and Jake's ex-wife were involved in a romantic relationship. Jake shook his head. Only in small-town America.

"Why would Kincaid care who Underwood is screwing?" Jake finally asked when he tapped the brakes as they approached the clinic.

"Duh." Dev leaned across the seat and swatted Jake's bicep. "Remember I told you that Poppy is in love with Noah."

"Do you really think she told her dad she was interested in Underwood and the chief is holding a grudge?" Jake raised a brow as he turned into the nearly empty parking lot and pulled into a spot near the door. He switched off the truck's engine and swiveled his head just in time to see Dev roll her eyes. "What?"

She freed herself from the seat belt and swung open the pickup's door. "My best friend may not have verbally admitted to her father that she loves Noah, but now that she and her dad mended their relationship and they're together more, I'm sure a trained officer of the law like the chief has figured it out."

Jake hurried around the Ford to help Dev to the

ground, but since he'd installed running boards, she no longer needed his assistance. Now she only waited for him when she was feeling frisky. In this situation, she was already out and heading toward the clinic.

He frowned. He missed picking her up and holding her close as he slowly slid her to the ground. Maybe those running boards would have to mysteriously disappear.

Jogging to catch up with Devereux, he barely beat her to the entrance and grabbed the handle. When the door wouldn't budge, he tapped on the glass. There was no response, and after a couple of minutes, he peered inside. However, the only thing he could see was an empty lobby.

Devereaux wrinkled her brow as she watched him. "This can't be good."

When he nodded his agreement, she dug into her purse and pulled out her cell. He wasn't happy to see that she had Underwood on speed dial, but he swallowed the flare of jealousy.

Devereaux had put the phone on speaker, and he could hear it ring and ring.

When it went to voicemail, Jake suggested, "Try the clinic number."

Dev nodded and brought up her contacts, then pressed the icon that dialed the number.

They both blew out a relieved breath when Meg's voice demanded, "Where are you two?"

Jake grabbed Devereaux's cell and snapped,

"Standing on the front step. You want to let us in?"

They heard the phone disconnect, and a few seconds later, Meg appeared in the foyer. She sprayed herself and the paper gowns, masks, gloves, and face shields that she was carrying with something from an aerosol can. She then cracked open the door and slid the protective equipment through the small gap.

Closing the door, she shouted, "Take off your coats and put this stuff on before you come inside." She narrowed her eyes and looked at Devereaux. "Leave your purse in the car."

Dev nodded, stuck her cell phone in her cleavage, and handed her jacket and bag to Jake. By the time he deposited it and the coats in the truck, she had on her gown. He hurriedly donned his gear. Meg then waved them through the door and relocked it once they were over the threshold.

While she herded them toward the clinic's front desk, she explained, "As soon as Noah realized our patient had been poisoned and that there was no indication that he had ingested or been injected with anything, he cleared the waiting room and put out a message that anything urgent should be taken to the ER."

Underwood met them near the check-in counter. He was similarly garbed in protective equipment and it was difficult to read his expression through the visor and mask.

Noah twisted his gloved hands as he said, "Thank goodness you're here. Mr. Burgess has gotten worse. When he first arrived, although he was agitated and having trouble breathing, he was coherent. Which is how I got consent to breach doctor-patient confidentiality and tell you what was happening. But now he's rambling and is experiencing miosis."

"Which is?" Jake asked.

Distractedly, Underwood rattled off the explanation, "Excessive constriction of the pupil of the eye."

"And you're sure these are signs of poisoning and not some other medical condition?" Jake asked.

"Absolutely," Noah sighed. "Mr. Burgess is perspiring excessively, incontinent, drooling, and his temperature is spiking. He has definitely somehow been exposed to a highly toxic chemical."

"Could it be a drug he willingly took to get high?" Devereaux asked.

"There are no inoculation sites on his body, and the friend who brought him into the clinic said Mr. Burgess had been on his tractor since eight this morning. This friend stopped around noon and brought him lunch, but that was the only time he left the fields."

"Could it have been in what he ate?" Jake asked.

"Do you think I'm an idiot?" Noah shouted, then regained his cool and said, "Symptoms like these wouldn't be from something he ingested orally. He had to have been exposed to something airborne or directly injected into his bloodstream."

"Shouldn't he be in a hospital?" Jake asked, then held up his hand to stop Underwood from blowing up at him again. "I know you're a good doctor, but this seems too serious for a clinic to handle."

"When he was first brought in, I gave him atropine, got him on breathing support and intravenous fluids, ordered blood and urine tests, a chest x-ray, ECG, then had the nurse wash him down and irrigate his eyes." Noah's tone was clinical, but then he frowned and added, "After I realized nothing was helping, I called for an ambulance, but all the nearby emergency vehicles are over at a multicar accident on the highway, and in his condition, he certainly can't be transported by car."

"So?" Jake frowned.

"The nearest available medical conveyance was forty-five minutes away. They should be here soon, but I was hoping you'd be able to talk to Mr. Burgess prior to their arrival."

"Okay." Jake hesitated, then pulled out his phone and swiped until he found what he wanted. "But before I do anything, I'll need you to sign this contract hiring my private detective services."

"You're worried about being paid?" Noah shot Devereaux a look that said, *This is who you chose over me.*

Jake growled, then forced himself to be calm and explained, "It's not about the money, it's about any legal ramifications that might occur."

"Fine!" Noah huffed. "Just get on with it."

Handing over his cell phone, Jake indicated where Underwood should sign, then grinned and said, "Now give me a dollar."

Dev prodded his arm and teased, "So it is about the money."

"Always." Jake trapped her poky finger and gently removed it from his bicep.

Once Underwood paid up, Jake looked at Devereaux and said, "Why don't you see if the guy who brought the vic in can tell us anything?"

"Mr. Escobar is in exam room two." Noah gestured down a short corridor. "In case he'd been contaminated too, I had him shower and gave him a set of scrubs, then isolated him."

"Okay, Underwood, lead me to your patient." Jake squeezed Dev's gloved hand, then followed Noah through a door marked with a number one. He approached the bed, but the man appeared comatose.

"Sir." Jake shook the guy's shoulder. "Can you tell me what happened to you?"

The man mumbled something and Jake leaned closer. Had Burgess just said he was attacked by a pterodactyl?

CHAPTER 4
Devereaux

I knocked lightly on the wooden door with a sign that read EXAMINATION 2. The little window was frosted, so I couldn't see inside, but this was the room Meg at shoved me towards so I assumed this was where they had stashed the victim's friend.

Knowing that Jake would want every little detail, and fearing that I would forget something important, as soon as a voice gave me permission to enter, I activated the recording app on my cell. Then I took a deep breath and opened the door.

There was an examination table, an uncomfortable-looking metal and vinyl chair, and a rolling stool. The guy I'd been assigned to interview was lying on the table with his arm covering his eyes. He was an attractive, darkly tanned man in his mid-thirties.

"Mr. Escobar, I'm Devereaux Sinclair. Dr. Underwood asked me to talk to you." I figured that was pretty close to the truth, and it might make the conversation easier.

"Is Aaron all right?" The man sat up and his dark brown eyes drilled into me. "No one will tell me anything."

"I don't believe there's been any change in Mr. Burgess's condition." Easing onto the stool, I sat down, arranging the bright aqua paper gown I wore around me. "Dr. Underwood said that the ambulance should be here very soon, and the ER will be more equipped to handle your friend's medical issues."

All those years I worked as a financial consultant came back to me as I avoided this guy's questions and spoke without really saying anything. I didn't miss my previous profession, even though I'd been forced out due to a crooked boss, but it was interesting to see that I hadn't lost my gift of gab.

"Call me Quito." Mr. Escobar rose from the table and held out his hand.

He was heavily muscled, and the scrubs that Noah had lent him pulled tightly across his biceps and thighs as he seated himself on the chair across from me.

"I'm Dev." We shook hands and smiled at each other, although I doubt that he could see my expression behind my mask or feel my palm through the rubber gloves, then I said, "It would be extremely helpful if you could tell me the circumstances leading up to you finding Mr. Burgess and realizing he wasn't feeling well. Do you work with your friend?"

Quito ran his fingers through his thick black hair. "Aaron and I were in the army together. When we got out, he talked me into moving here and partnering up with him to run the family farm. He'd inherited twenty-five hundred acres from his father, and it was too much for one person to manage alone."

"Is it just the two of you?"

"Mostly." Quito fiddled with the drawstring tie on his pants. "We hire out when needed, but because of all the rain earlier this spring, everyone's way behind in planting, so there was no one available, and we were really busting our humps to get all the seed in."

"That's tough." I nodded sympathetically. "My family used to farm, but we ended up having to sell the land because we just couldn't make a living from it."

Again, what I was telling him was mostly true. But we'd actually had to sell because my gran had needed the money to survive.

"We've been doing okay, but we certainly couldn't afford to lose any of our potential crop." Quito leaned his elbows on his knees. "Aaron and I have been working sixteen-hour days. We both might have all our money tied up in the farm, but it's Aaron's family's land, so I knew he was pushing himself too hard. He wasn't even stopping to eat, so I brought him lunch."

"That was really nice of you." I made sure

approval came across in my voice since he couldn't really see my expression behind the mask that I was wearing.

"It wasn't a big deal." Quito's darkly tanned cheeks reddened. "My trailer is about halfway between the field where I was working and the one that Aaron was at, so I just stopped, threw some meat and cheese between some slices of bread, grabbed a package of potato chips and a couple of drinks."

"Did you and Mr. Burgess eat the same thing?" I knew Noah had said it couldn't be the lunch, but there was no harm in checking.

"Yeah. Ham and swiss on rye with potato chips and a can of orange soda." Quito's gaze was quizzical. "Does the doc think he has food poisoning?"

"I don't believe so," I assured him. "Do you feel sick?"

"Nope." He wrinkled his forehead and his thick black brows met over his nose. "But I would like my stuff back. I just got those boots broke in right."

I was pretty sure Noah wasn't planning to give Quito his clothes back. At least not until he found out what was causing Mr. Burgess's symptoms, but I'd leave it up to him to share that little tidbit of news.

Instead, I asked, "How did Mr. Burgess seem when you two had lunch together?"

"Fine." Quito rubbed the dark stubble on his chin. "Happy that we were making good progress with the planting."

"What else did you guys talk about?"

"Uh." Quito scratched his head. "Mostly work stuff. Although, I did tell him that I was knocking off early. I had originally planned to take the whole day off because I had a date in the city, but I decided to work a few hours."

"Why's that?"

"I just realized that as long as I was on the road no later than five, I would be fine." Quito twitched his shoulders. "Anyway, after we talked about me cutting out around four, Aaron mentioned his wife had left that morning and would be gone until Monday night, so he'd work until dark."

"Was it unusual for her to travel without him?" I wondered if Noah had contacted Mrs. Burgess or even realized that she existed.

"Nah. Rose's a flight attendant, so she's away nine or ten days a month."

"What time did you finish lunch?" I was trying to get the chronology straight.

"Let's see." Quito half closed his eyes. "We were together from a little after noon to around twelve thirty, then I went back to where I was working."

"What made you return to where Mr. Burgess was planting?" I couldn't recall if Noah had told us exactly when Quito brought in his friend, but if the ambulance was due any minute, I guessed that they'd been there an hour or so, which would make it between two thirty and three when they arrived.

"When I finished up the field I was working in, I

couldn't find my phone. I checked the cab of my tractor, my house, and my truck, but no luck. The only other place that I'd been was with Aaron for lunch, so I figured I'd dropped it over there."

I pulled up a mental picture of the rural area around Shadow Bend. "Where is Mr. Burgess's and your land located?"

"It's about ten miles east of town off Viridine Road." Quito hiked a thumb in what I assumed was that general direction.

I tried to picture the geography involved, but I couldn't. "What happened when you got to that spot?" Jake and I would have to take a ride and see it for ourselves.

"The tractor was stopped in the middle of the field, and Aaron was slumped over the wheel." Quito's olive complexion paled. "I ran out to him and he was barely conscious. He didn't even recognize me, and he was shaking so bad I half dragged, half carried him to my truck. Then I hauled ass to Doc Underwood's clinic."

"Because it was closer?" I murmured. The nearest hospital was an hour from Shadow Bend and even farther from some of the farms.

Quito opened his mouth to answer me but snapped it shut when we both heard a siren getting closer and closer.

"That must be—"

Before I could finish my sentence, he jumped to

his feet and ran out the door, shouting over his shoulder, "Sorry. I gotta go with Aaron to the hospital."

CHAPTER 5
Devereux

Noah, Meg, Jake, and I watched the ambulance race out of the clinic's parking lot. Once it was gone, we trooped into the waiting room and fell, exhausted, into the uncomfortable black vinyl chairs.

Noah groaned, then looked between Jake and me and asked, "Did you two find out anything helpful?"

"Not unless you think a pterodactyl might have poisoned the guy." Jake smirked. "That was all Burgess said to me."

"His hallucinations must have gotten worse." Noah ran his fingers through his dark blond hair, then turned his attention to me. "Anything from Mr. Escobar?"

I played the recording that I'd made of our conversation, then said, "So it would seem whatever happened to Mr. Burgess, occurred between twelve thirty and whatever time Quito got here."

"I think he came in a little after three," Noah

offered.

Meg had been strangely quiet since we'd arrived. She hadn't even tried to annoy me by flirting with Jake, which was highly unusual.

Now she seemed to perk up and said, "Three seventeen to be exact." Then when we all stared at her, she shrugged and said, "What? I write down the time the patient approaches the desk, and I have a good memory."

I nodded, then asked, "Was Mr. Burgess's wife notified?"

"Shit!" Noah's smoky gray eyes clouded, and he thunked his head against the back of the chair. "I didn't think to inquire whether he was married."

Meg flipped her long red hair over her shoulder, reached for Noah's hand, and said, "We were all overwhelmed." She shot an exasperated glance at me. "The clinic isn't really equipped to deal with this type of extreme emergency."

I held up my palms. "I wasn't suggesting that there had been any negligence."

"You better not," Meg muttered under her breath.

Not surprisingly, Jake's ex wasn't my biggest fan. Which was fine. Because I didn't like her either. Not only had she dumped Jake when it looked as if he might end up in a wheelchair, she'd pretended she was sick even after she'd recovered in an attempt to get me to break up with him. And to top it all off, she'd swooped down on Noah before I could persuade Poppy to tell him that she was in love with him.

Pushing aside my animosity toward Meg, I said, "Quito mentioned that his clothes had been confiscated. I'm guessing that applies to Mr. Burgess's, as well."

"Yes. Why?" Meg crossed her arms in a practiced move that emphasized her large breasts. She shot me an ice-pick smile when she saw that I had noticed her behavior.

I knew for a fact her boobs were cosmetically enhanced to the tune of six thousand dollars. Jake was still seething that, during the last few days of their marriage, she had used their joint account to pay for her vanity.

Jake said that Meg always liked to push the envelope to see what would shake out. I had replied that no matter how much you shoved at it, it would still be stationery.

Finally answering Meg's question, I said, "Maybe their cell phones could tell us something." I shrugged. "At the very least, they'd probably give us a way to contact Mrs. Burgess."

Noah straightened and glanced at Meg. "I know we sent Mr. Burgess's belongings with him in a sealed bag in the ambulance, with a note that the contents might be contaminated, but what happened to Mr. Escobar's possessions?"

"He ran out of here so fast he didn't ask about them." Meg jumped up and scurried into the back, returning seconds later with a large white plastic drawstring bag imprinted with the words UNDERWOOD CLINIC.

Jake held out his hand. "I wish I would have had a chance to search Burgess's stuff, but let me take a look at Escobar's."

Meg narrowed her green eyes and clasped the bag to her chest. She took a step backward and stared at Jake as if daring him to try for it.

Noah shook his head and sighed. "Just give it to him, Meg."

"Here." She thrust the sack at Jake, then resumed her seat next to Noah.

While Jake examined the contents of the bag, Noah sighed. "I need to call in a company to sanitize this place before Monday morning. Thank goodness we're dark on Sundays."

I had forgotten it was Saturday. Usually, I'd be at the dime store. It was one of our busiest days since we closed at four and didn't open up again until noon on Monday.

Due to my moving in with Jake and Tony moving in with Gran, my father was covering my shift. I hoped Dad hadn't been too overwhelmed. Even though he'd been working for me for the past eight or so months, previously I'd only left him in charge on a few occasions.

Jake interrupted my thoughts when he said to Noah, "I'll text you the number of a company that can handle biohazardous materials." He took out his phone and swiped the screen. "Maybe by the time they get out here, the hospital will have identified the toxin."

"We can only hope." Noah's doubtful expression was not reassuring.

Jake finished his search of Quito's personal effects and said, "Besides his clothes, the only things in his pocket were his wallet, keys, and a comb. And there's nothing in the wallet except his driver's license, credit cards, and cash. Nothing helpful or that tells us how to contact his friend's wife. I guess he never found his cell phone."

"Shoot!" Noah's lips pressed together. "I'd better call the hospital and figure out how to get Mr. Escobar his possessions. We'll keep the clothes and wipe down the rest. He'll need his wallet and keys."

"Dev and I will drop them off and give him a ride back here to pick up his truck. I have one or two more questions for Escobar, so that will give me time to talk to him." Jake shot a look at Noah. "That is, if you want me to continue looking into this matter. Depending on what the hospital finds regarding Burgess's poisoning, my guess is that they'll call in the county sheriff. We can end the contract if you'd rather leave it in the hands of the authorities."

Noah shook his head, a stubborn look on his face. "I highly doubt that local deputies have ever seen anything like this or have a clue how to figure it out. Keep investigating. Monday afternoon, I'll drop a check off at your office to cover your retainer."

"Okay." Jake stood and I followed suit.

Noah got to his feet too. "Fingers crossed, whatever affected Mr. Burgess doesn't seem to have contaminated those around him or this immediate environment. However, just in case, we should probably get out of here and not risk any further exposure."

"Quito said he felt fine," I offered. "That has to be a good sign since he had the most exposure."

"Probably," Noah hedged. "But when he first came in, he was twitching and said he'd vomited. Once we got him out of his clothes and showered, he started feeling better."

"By the way, what did you do with the rest of your staff?" I asked.

"As soon as I realized what we might be dealing with here, I got everyone into personal protective equipment." Noah swept his hand around the room. "Then I sent home all the patients waiting to be seen and told Yale and Eunice to leave too."

Yale Gordon was Noah's physician assistant, and Eunice Vogel was his head nurse. I was a bit surprised that Eunice had left. She was fiercely loyal to Noah and regarded him almost as her son. She would have usually stayed until the bitter end.

My guess was that she and Meg had become rivals for his attention, and the young, pretty redhead probably beat the motherly blonde hands down. I stole a peek at Meg, who stared back at me with a smug smile on her face as if she could read my mind.

"Dr. Rodriguez wasn't working today?" Jake asked.

"No, Elexus is out of town." Noah slumped in his chair. "She had some personal crises, so I've been on my own."

Elexus Rodriguez was Noah's new partner. She'd joined the practice last October, and Monday through Saturday, she and Noah alternated covering the two shifts—seven a.m. to one p.m. and one p.m. to six p.m.

It had been a good arrangement for both doctors. For Noah, it allowed him some free time, and for Elexus, who had only recently finished her residency, it gave her some much-needed practical experience.

I was wondering what Dr. Rodriguez's emergency had been when Noah broke into my thoughts as he said, "I'd be happy to treat you both to dinner if you want to meet up at the Golden Dragon after you bring Mr. Escobar back to his truck."

"I'm sure Dev doesn't want Jake to spend any more time around me than he already has." Meg's voice was so caustic she could have used it to etch metal.

Jake ignored her and gave my hand a squeeze. "We have plans. Right?"

"Definitely!" I beamed at him, more than ready to get away from Jake's ex.

"Okay, then. I'll see you in your office tomorrow."

Jake nodded to Noah, slung an arm around my

shoulder, and headed toward the door.

CHAPTER 6
Devereaux

"Remind me about how Underwood ended up opening the clinic." Jake glanced at me as he drove us to County General Hospital.

"What do you mean?" I turned slightly and studied his profile.

"Did he work anywhere else or…" Jake trailed off as he approached a slow-moving tractor and had to apply the pickup's brakes.

"He always wanted to be a small-town doctor," I answered thoughtfully, recalling our talks when we were dating in high school.

Noah's desire to serve his community had been one of the things that I admired most about him. Well, that and his smoking-hot good looks.

"Where did he go to medical school?" Jake's expression was bland, but I wasn't fooled.

Narrowing my eyes, I said, "Noah was accepted at Harvard, Duke, and a couple other top-notch universities, but due to his mother's health, he did the combined BA and MD program at the University of Missouri, then a three-year residency in family medicine in St. Louis. Why do you ask?"

"Just checking that he didn't get his degree at some offshore med school." Jake shrugged. "I was halfway hoping he might have missed something obvious with Burgess, and that when we get to the hospital, the docs there would have a handle on the poison."

"That could happen," I conceded, then added, "But only because they have more access to equipment and lab results than Noah's clinic."

"Speaking of Underwood's clinic, did he fund it himself?" Jake was finally able to overtake the combine and immediately brought his truck up to speed.

"Probably." I had never asked him. "Of Shadow Bend's five founding families, the Underwoods are by far the wealthiest." I snickered. "And the Sinclairs are the poorest."

"If Underwood's as smart a guy as you say," Jake mused, "you'd think he'd want more of a challenge than just being a small-town doc."

"Oh, I think being the only medical provider within an hour's drive is pretty challenging."

"Maybe."

"Well, one time, when Noah and I were discussing my old job, where I had to drive into Kansas City every day, he said that he'd never be able to stand the horrendous commute." I laughed. "He joked that with his road rage, he'd probably end up shooting someone, which wouldn't do his kindly doctor image any good."

Instead of chuckling, which was what I expected, Jake made a noncommittal sound. But the scowl on his face said that he wasn't amused.

I fidgeted with my seat belt. Was Jake projecting his own frustrations at being stuck in the middle of nowhere after the exciting life he led as a US Marshal? Or was this more a case of jealousy? If so, I sure hoped it was over my past relationship with Noah and not his ex-wife's current one.

Never one to shy away from the hard questions, I cleared my throat and asked, "So what do you think of Meg and Noah as a couple?"

"They're a weird combo, but if it keeps her out of my hair, I'm all for it." Jake slid me a quick appraising look. "What do you think?"

"I think he and Poppy would be a better match." I bit my lip. "But when I suggested she tell him how she felt about him, she insisted that she didn't want to be his rebound romance."

"Rebound from you?"

"Yeah." I picked at my nails, which were overdue for a manicure. "I can sort of see her point."

For a while, I had dated both Jake and Noah. Finally, last October, I'd realized that while I would always love Noah, I wasn't in love with him and the emotion that I felt for him was more an echo from our past puppy love than the real feelings that I had for Jake.

Jake tapped my nose. "Meg does make the perfect person for a rebound relationship."

I barely kept my voice level. "Really?" What the heck did he mean by that?

"Look at it this way. Underwood wouldn't have any trouble finding a girl for his rebound, but he might have trouble getting rid of her once they got past the honeymoon phase."

"True." I nodded. "He's not very good about breaking up with people, and we can only assume that eventually Meg will tire of him and small-town life and move on. I sure can't see her settling down to be the doctor's wife."

"What I really wonder"—Jake crinkled his brow—"is why Meg's still sticking around Shadow Bend, working as a receptionist."

"I agree. Her skill set does seem underutilized in her current position." It was my turn to shoot an appraising look at Jake. "Do you think she's trying to get you back?"

"Not in a million years." Jake chuckled. "Although, she's always enjoyed creating drama, so I'm sure she loves causing any friction she can in our relationship."

Stretching across the bench seat, I kissed Jake's cheek. "Let's not give her that pleasure."

"Deal." Jake squeezed my thigh, then returned

his hand to the wheel as he exited onto the state road that led to the hospital.

With Jake's attention on the increasing traffic, I took out my phone and sent a couple of quick texts to my two best friends. In addition to being the police chief's daughter, Poppy Kinkaid owned Gossip Central. It was the most popular club in a hundred-mile radius, and she had the place bugged so she could monitor the hot topics of the day.

My other BFF, Boone St. Onge, was Shadow Bend's premiere attorney. While he didn't resort to Poppy's methods, between his law practice and his eligible bachelor status, he probably heard more of the townspeople's secrets than our local priest, Father Flagg, did during confession.

I figured if there were any rumors floating around about Aaron Burgess, Poppy or Boone would have heard them. And if Aaron's condition was truly due to a deliberate action, their information might give us a place to start the investigation.

While I waited for Poppy and Boone to respond to my message, I gazed out the window, then chuckled.

"What's so funny?" Jake shot me a confused look.

"The sign on the church back there." I gestured behind us.

Jake took a quick glance in the rearview mirror, then gave up and asked, "What did it say?"

I recited, "Adam and Eve were the first people

not to read the apple terms and conditions."

He laughed and added, "And they certainly won't be the last."

CHAPTER 7
Devereaux

As Jake turned into the hospital parking lot and pulled into a spot close to the main entrance, I congratulated myself on obtaining my Missouri private investigator's license. Now that I was official, I could legally work with Jake solving cases. And Aaron Burgess's poisoning might be the biggest mystery we'd run across yet.

Jake had instructed Noah to call the hospital and have Quito meet us at the reception desk so that we could return his belongings. I hoped when we saw him, he would have good news about his friend's condition. But from what I could gather from Noah's hedging and medical jargon, Mr. Burgess's prognosis wasn't good.

However, even with the odds against a positive outcome for the ailing farmer, I was still optimistic as Jake and I walked through the hospital door. There was just something soothing about the quiet, softly lit interior that inspired confidence.

After all, Noah wasn't infallible. If he was, he wouldn't be dating Meg.

Tamping down my smile at that last thought, I looked around the lobby. In truth, I was surprised that it *was* so peaceful. I had been expecting chaos like on television.

Oh, right! Those programs were mostly set in the ER or the ICU. We were where visitors were greeted, not where accident victims and the seriously wounded were brought for treatment.

It might seem odd that I had never been in a hospital before and was therefore reacting to this experience as if I were on some high school field trip, but Gran was remarkably healthy for her age. And with no close relatives or older friends in the area, I had managed to avoid the place until now.

Even when Tony had broken his hip, he'd only been held overnight for his injury. And instead of going with Jake to see him then, I'd had to stay home with Birdie. Her elderly beau's accident had upset her to the point that she couldn't function on her own.

However, now that I was experiencing my first visit to the hospital, I had to admit, I was a little…not disappointed, but maybe let down. The scene before me looked more like a mid-level hotel than a place of life or death.

Shaking my head at how silly I was being, I gazed around the tranquil lobby and frowned. There was no sign of Quito.

Jake and I walked along the high-backed chairs, elegant sofas, and glass and steel end tables scattered around the room, checking for him. When we'd covered the entire room, he and I exchanged puzzled glances. Where was he?

Taking my arm, Jake steered me toward the reception desk. The woman who greeted us was probably in her fifties, but it was hard to tell with the amount of makeup she was wearing.

The badge attached to the lapel of her tweed jacket read MS. PRICE. She looked up from her keyboard with a frown, but as she eyed Jake, it quickly turned into a smile.

Tilting her head to a coquettish angle, she asked, "May I help you?"

"I believe Dr. Underwood contacted you concerning Mr. Escobar." Jake leaned an elbow on the counter.

Ms. Price's smile grew larger. "He did indeed. I understand you have some of Mr. Escobar's things. Items that were mistakenly left at Dr. Underwood's clinic when Mr. Escobar's friend was transported to our ER."

"That's correct." Jake held up the plastic bag he'd been carrying. "Mr. Escobar was supposed to meet us here."

"Hmm." Ms. Price gazed past us and pointed at a chair near the door. "That's odd. The last time I looked, he was sitting over there. He was very anxious to get his possessions back and didn't want to miss you."

"Maybe he went to the bathroom." I nudged the sack in Jake's hand. "We have his wallet, and his truck is still at the clinic, so he couldn't have gone too far away."

"Let me check to see if he was called to be with his friend." Ms. Price picked up the phone and punched a few numbers.

She asked about Quito. An instant later, her glance bounced up from the phone to Jake's face, then she turned her back and held a hushed conversation with whoever was on the other end of the line.

While she was talking, I whispered to Jake, "That doesn't look good."

Ms. Price hung up the receiver and said, "I'm afraid Mr. Escobar has been taken to the sheriff's department to answer some questions. I'm not sure if he'll be returning here or not. The deputy who escorted him didn't indicate what would happen next."

"How is Mr. Burgess?" I asked, not expecting her to answer me but wanting to see her reaction.

"He didn't…" The receptionist trailed off, then said, "I mean I really can't release that information."

We nodded our understanding and Jake said, "I guess we'll bring Escobar's stuff to the sheriff's office."

He was silent as we walked to the exit. Sensing he didn't want anyone to overhear our conversation, I remained quiet until we got to where he'd parked the truck.

When we were both seated inside the pickup, I asked, "Why do think the deputy took Quito away?"

"If Burgess is in deed dead, as the receptionist's behavior suggests, then his cause of death is suspicious, and Escobar was the one who found him." Jake spared me a glance as he drove down the quiet residential street. "We need to figure out how to play this."

"What do you mean?" Although I asked, I had a good idea what he was thinking, and I didn't like where he was going.

"It's probably best that we do some recon before local law enforcement realize that Underwood hired me." Jake paused as he came to the road leading to the sheriff's office. Once he made the turn, he continued, "Would you be okay with taking Escobar's stuff into the sheriff's office by yourself? You can let them think you work for Underwood."

Jake was asking me if I was comfortable going in alone because, when we'd first met, I'd been a little paranoid about entering the local police station. Its square cinder-block building, barred front windows, and overall oppressive atmosphere had reminded me of the prison where my dad had spent twelve of the past thirteen years.

The resemblance had been a problem for me because during my one and only visit to the penitentiary while my father was in residence, I had developed a sort of claustrophobia that kicked in whenever I stepped into anything that resembled a jail. If I thought too long about being locked up, I tended to lose the ability to breathe.

Since my dad had been freed, I'd gotten a lot better about being inside law enforcement facilities, but it still made me a bit light-headed, and in my experience, fainting rarely left a good impression on a cop. No matter how much I denied it, they tended to believe alcohol was involved.

I was still mulling over my answer to Jake's request when we arrived at the sheriff's office. It was located downtown at the rear of the courthouse. The lot behind the building was for police vehicles and employees only, which meant parking for everyone else was at the meters lining the street.

Luckily, it was not only the weekend, but well past normal business hours, so there was an abundance of spaces. Jake swung smoothly into the slot nearest the entrance, and looked at me.

When I remained staring at the intimidating structure, Jake took my hand and said, "It's okay if you'd rather not."

Looking to his concerned blue eyes, I took a deep breath and said, "No problem." I forced a smile and said, "I told Quito that Noah wanted me to talk to him, so if I happen to see him, he shouldn't blow my cover."

Jake kissed my knuckles, gave my fingers a final

squeeze, released my hand, and fished a quarter from the among the change in one of the truck's cupholders. Accepting the coin, I pasted on a brave smile, grabbed the plastic bag with Quito's belongings, and climbed out of the truck.

After feeding the meter, I walked toward the building. With every step I took, my chest tightened, and I had to remind myself to breathe as I pushed open the door. The lobby was silent and empty, and I concentrated on inhaling and exhaling in order to remain vertical as I crossed toward the counter.

The young man behind bulletproof glass was laughing into the telephone, but the minute he caught sight of me, he muttered a quick goodbye and tossed the receiver onto the cradle.

"May I help you?" He spoke through an intercom.

"The hospital told me that Quito Escobar might be here." I held up the plastic bag. "He left some of his stuff at the Underwood Clinic, and I'd like to return it to him."

"Let me check." The young man, who, according to the tag pinned to his long-sleeved blue polo shirt, was named Tim Benjamin, picked up the phone and turned his back on me.

That didn't seem like a good sign. I leaned forward, but I couldn't hear a thing.

A few seconds later, my pulse sped up when a middle-aged man in uniform stepped through an interior door. I assumed it led into the rest of the building, and I'd bet my slice of Gran's next chocolate pie that there were jail cells back there.

My heart was thudding so loudly I almost couldn't hear it when the man said, "I'm Deputy Riggs. I understand you're a friend of Mr. Escobar."

"No." I shook my head. "I'm just doing Dr. Underwood a favor since he felt so bad about forgetting to return Quito's possessions before he accompanied his friend to the hospital."

"How did the doctor come to have Mr. Escobar's property?" Deputy Riggs wrinkled his brow.

"Dr. Underwood had him undress because he was afraid that he'd been contaminated—"

"This sounds complicated," the deputy stopped me. "Let's sit down."

I wanted to protest, but I wasn't sure how to get out of this situation without bringing even more attention to myself. It was probably best to just cooperate and tell as much of the truth as possible.

Evidently noticing my hesitation, the deputy motioned me through the door. When I reluctantly complied, he led me into an empty office.

Once we were settled in chairs facing the desk, the deputy smoothed his short salt-and-pepper hair and said, "Let's start with your identity."

"Devereaux Sinclair."

I watched as his hazel eyes narrowed as if trying to remember where he'd heard my name before. I held my breath. My father's conviction had been splashed all over the papers. Of course, when the facts about his innocence surfaced, that event was not as widely covered.

Thankfully, the deputy didn't seem to connect me to the scandal surrounding my dad's incarceration, and after a few seconds, he shrugged and said, "You mentioned that the doctor had Mr. Escobar disrobe due to fear of contamination, of what exactly?"

"That was the problem." I put the bag I was still holding on the desk. "Dr. Underwood wasn't sure what had caused Mr. Burgess's condition, so he was being cautious."

"Hmm." Deputy Riggs tapped the plastic sack. "And when the victim was transported to the hospital, Mr. Escobar accompanied him and, in all the commotion, forgot his things. How did that happen?"

"When the ambulance finally arrived, Mr. Escobar rushed to be with his friend. I'm guessing the fact that all he had on were scrubs was the furthest thing from his mind." Afraid that I'd slip and reveal that I had been questioning Quito at the time, I decided to ask my own question. "How is Mr. Burgess?"

The deputy stared at me as if considering his reply, then said, "I'm sorry to say that he passed away about an hour ago."

"That's terrible." Judging from the hospital receptionist's behavior, we'd been pretty sure that had been the case, but I was still saddened to hear it confirmed. "Did the ER know what caused his death?" When the deputy shot me a suspicious look, I hastily added, "Dr. Underwood will want to know."

"The ER doc had a few ideas, but we'll have to wait until the autopsy to confirm them." Deputy Riggs rubbed the back of his neck. "The only thing he was sure about was that it wasn't natural causes."

"Dr. Underwood didn't think so either." I got up, more than ready to leave. "You should give him a call. He'd know a lot more than I do about the whole situation. I'm really just a messenger."

"Do you work for Dr. Underwood?"

Shoot! I had been trying to avoid that question. What should I say?

"No." I could hardly lie about that as it would be easy to find out the truth. "He and his girlfriend were supposed to have dinner with my fiancé and me." That would be a lot more difficult to disprove. "Jake and I stopped at the clinic to pick them up, but of course, with everything that happened, Noah and Meg begged off our double date."

Phew! That was walking a fine line.

"Why would you volunteer to drop off Mr. Escobar's things?" Deputy Riggs stared at me.

"Just to help out a friend." I shrugged. "Noah felt really bad about Mr. Escobar being without his wallet and keys."

"I see." Deputy Riggs grabbed a Post-it and pencil and shoved them toward me. "Give me the doc's cell number."

I took out my phone and copied Noah's number onto the bright yellow square, deliberately transposing the last two digits. There was no way I wanted the deputy to contact Noah before I could get in touch with him and brief him on our cover story.

As the deputy tucked away the slip of paper, I nudged the plastic bag and asked, "Is Mr. Escobar here?"

"Yes." Deputy Riggs got to his feet. "I'll see that he gets this before we release him."

"Great." I couldn't wait to get out of the building and quickly retraced my steps toward the lobby.

Deputy Riggs followed me. I hoped he wouldn't continue with me outside.

"Thank you for your help." He pushed open the glass door.

"No problem." Although I wanted to run, I strolled out and even managed to make myself turn and wave at the deputy, who was watching me from the doorway.

He waved back, and when he finally turned away, I sprinted for the truck.

Leaping inside, I said, "Get us out of here now."

Jake shot me a concerned glance but turned on the ignition and reversed onto the road.

As we headed toward home, I hurriedly texted Noah about what he needed to tell the deputy regarding why Jake and I were at the clinic.

Once I was finished, I looked at Jake and said,

"Next time, it's your turn in the hotseat."

CHAPTER 8
Devereaux

It was nearly eight by the time we got back to the ranch. Poppy and Boone still hadn't responded to my texts, and I was getting a little worried. I could understand the delay with Poppy — Saturday nights at Gossip Central were a madhouse — but Boone hadn't mentioned having any plans, and he normally answered me right away.

While earlier I had been stuffed from the huge lunch that Gran had fed us, now my stomach was growling louder than that lion that introduced all those old movies. Jake had suggested stopping at a restaurant before we left the county seat, but I was bound and determined to go ahead with our plans for a romantic supper at home.

The minute Jake stopped the truck, I said, "I'm starving. I'll get the Weber going."

I leaped out of the pickup and raced around to the back deck. After firing up the gas grill, I returned to the front of the house just in time for Jake to unlock and open the door.

Allowing me to precede him inside, he asked, "What do you want me to do?"

That was one of the reasons that I loved this guy. No snide comments about my appetite and ready to help out any way that he could.

"Shower in the guest bath, put on a new outfit, and leave your jeans and shirt in the laundry room." I ticked off his duties on my fingers, then added, "Once you're done with that, cook the steaks."

I headed into the master bath determined to shed any vestige of contamination I might have picked up at Noah's clinic. Although we'd both been wearing protective gear, I still wanted to get our clothes in the washer ASAP. It was also important that we clean off anything that might linger on our skin or hair.

Fifteen minutes later, I was chopping veggies for our salad while I watched my fiancé—I loved that word—through the back door. Wearing the charcoal-gray lounge pants that I'd bought him for Valentine's Day, he placed huge rib-eyes on the grill.

The matching black V-neck thermal shirt stretched tight across his biceps as he opened and closed a pair of tongs. He stood over the steaks, poised to flip them at just the right moment.

Drooling a little at both the aroma of the sizzling meat and the sight of my tasty fiancé, I was glad that I'd put on my nicest leggings with a flowy peach cashmere tunic. I wanted to look as good to him as he did to me.

When I saw Jake turn the rib-eyes, I pushed the microwave's on button, and while the potatoes cooked, I moved to my next task. Placing napkins, silverware, butter, and sour cream on a tray, I brought them into the family room and arranged them on the coffee table facing the fireplace.

It was chilly in the house, so I tried to remember the lessons Jake had given me on lighting a fire. First, I placed two medium-sized pieces of wood on the metal grate about a hand's width apart. Then I crumpled sheets of newspaper in between them, covered that with kindling, and added two more logs.

I paused, tapping my chin. There was something else important that I was supposed to do.

Right! Check that the damper was fully open.

Once I was sure that I wasn't about to fill the room with smoke, I twisted a sheet of newspaper, struck a match, and held it to the impromptu torch. Using its flame to light the kindling, I waited until I saw a good blaze before stepping back.

By the time I heard the microwave beep, I had a nice fire going, and with one last admiring glance at my handwork, I hurried into the kitchen. Jake joined me a few minutes later, and after we both got our drinks and loaded our plates, we settled on the floor behind the coffee table. The sofa made a perfect backrest.

Jake put his arm around me, and I snuggled into

the cup of his shoulder. This was exactly how I had pictured our evening going—only in my imagination our romantic dinner had taken place a whole lot earlier.

Sighing in contentment, I studied my fiancé. Jake seemed to get better and better looking. His thick ebony hair curled over the collar of his thermal shirt, making me want to run my fingers through the silky strands. And his full lips tempted me to climb onto his lap and forget the food. What could one little kiss, or ten, hurt?

Before I could carry out my plan, my stomach growled. I really did need to eat or I'd be swooning for a reason that didn't involve my fiancé's attractiveness.

"Oops!" I felt my cheeks redden.

"No worries." Jake's sapphire eyes twinkled with laughter. "I'm hungry too."

I sat up and grabbed my fork and knife. "I guess we better have dinner before everything gets cold."

We dug in to the meal, and the only sounds for quite a while were my moans of enjoyment. There was absolutely nothing better than a steak from your own herd that had been grilled to perfection by your own cowboy.

Once we had sated our appetite, Jake drained his beer bottle and said, "Let's grab our dessert and a cup of coffee."

"Sounds wonderful." I followed him into the kitchen and opened Gran's pie saver.

While I sliced the tart, I watched as Jake

measured grounds into the coffeepot. His striking blue eyes were fringed with dense black lashes, and wisps of dark hair curled against the V of his shirt.

Even performing mundane tasks, he had an air of authority. I never dreamed that I would fall in love with such an alpha kind of guy. I thought my taste ran more to betas like Noah. But I really loved that Jake was someone who wouldn't take shit from anyone, even me, and that he didn't care what people thought of him.

It wasn't as if he'd ever tried to order me around. Or on the rare occasion that he did, he wasn't at all surprised when I ignored him. The attraction to his confident manner was more because I could relax, knowing that I didn't have to worry about every little thing anymore, than because I had any desire to have someone take over my life. What I liked was having someone to share the burden.

After we returned to the family room and settled on the sofa, Jake said, "I'm real proud of you going into the sheriff's office and handling the deputy so well."

"Me too." I sipped my coffee. "It's interesting that the ER doc didn't know what killed Aaron Burgess."

"Even more so that the deputy still had Escobar in custody." Jake dug into his tart.

"Yeah." I nibbled a walnut; the delicious dessert suddenly didn't seem as appealing. "I feel sorry for Quito. He appeared to be genuinely concerned about his friend and tried to help him, and now he's a suspect in that friend's death."

"The cops usually go for the most obvious person." The bronze skin tightened over his cheekbones, and Jake muttered, "I'm glad Underwood texted me that he wants us to continue to investigate, because my gut tells me this case is anything but predictable."

CHAPTER 9
Jake

Jake slipped quietly out of bed, grabbed his clothes, and tiptoed into the adjoining bathroom. He pulled on his jeans, then slid his arms into a blue flannel shirt. The material was worn to the exact point that he liked it—soft as a second skin but still thick enough to keep out the cold.

There was no sense in showering before he dressed. He'd only get dirty as he worked. It might be Sunday, but that didn't mean a day off when you managed a cattle ranch. There were always cattle to feed and chores to be done.

Once he put on socks and buckled his belt, Jake returned to the bedroom and leaned down to kiss Devereaux. He stopped, a hairsbreadth from her cheek, and stared at the beautiful woman who had agreed to be his wife.

He gently brushed a cinnamon-colored curl behind her ear and inhaled the smell of her spicy yet sweet perfume. It lingered in the air around her like a promise of everything good in the world.

Although he couldn't see them, he pictured her pretty blue-green eyes smiling at him as they had during their fireside dinner. The expression on her face as she gazed at him made his heart thud so strongly it felt as if it would burst out of his chest.

Since meeting Devereaux, he'd asked himself a million times why he'd ever married Meg. It was difficult to remember why he'd ever thought she was the one for him. How had he believed that he'd loved her? It had to have been the shared adrenaline of the job and the ignorance of youth.

With one last glance at his gorgeous fiancée, Jake crept out of the bedroom. He walked through the kitchen and into the mudroom, where he leaned against the wall and pulled his Durangos on over his stocking feet.

Heading outside, Jake thought about last night. They'd retired early, both of them tired from the move and being pulled in to investigate Burgess's death.

Devereaux had gotten ready for bed while he'd gone through the house, making sure the doors were locked and the lights were out. Unfortunately, by the time he'd returned to the master bedroom and crawled between the covers, she was already fast asleep.

Although he'd been hoping for some loving, he didn't have the heart to wake her. Devereaux always managed to light his fuse, but this time the explosion had to be delayed. And strangely, he'd been as content holding her in his arms while he drifted off to dreamland as he would have been launching his rocket.

It dawned on him. Those feelings must be the difference between true love and fleeting lust.

Chuckling to himself at his deep thoughts, Jake strode over to the detached garage and approached the UTV. Slinging his leg over the side, he winced.

When the docs told him that his injury was healed, they'd warned him that he'd always have some pain. And after hauling all of Tony's possessions over to Birdie's yesterday, his knee was bothering him more than usual.

He probably should have hired someone to help with the heavy lifting, but his pride had gotten in the way. Now he was paying the price.

Ignoring the twinge, Jake drove off to check that the fences around the south pasture had been mended. Once he made his rounds, he'd return and help the hands with the feeding.

In the fifty years Tony had been ranching, he had bought up a lot of neighboring property. Now they had a vast acreage of native grass ranges and grazing paddocks, as well as a small field of feed corn to use as an energy supplement for the cows. But until the weather improved, the herd would still need hay.

As Jake passed the covered corrals, he pictured them next week when they'd be full of Del Vecchio cows ready to be shipped. The ranch was primarily a cow/calf operation, but they also raised and sold replacement heifers, as well as sourcing product to local restaurants in the immediate area and in Kansas City.

Which reminded him, he was scheduled to meet with Cameron Niall, a chef from a new place, at one o'clock.

Shoot! He'd been hoping to get the chores done early and spend the rest of the day with Devereaux investigating Burgess's mysterious death.

Best-case scenario, the chef was gone by two or three, and they could still take a run over to see the area where the vic had been working when he was poisoned. Worst-case, the guy would stick around all afternoon.

Jake rode the fence line for half an hour. His two ranch hands had done a good job with the latest round of repairs, and he was about to head back when he noticed his nearest neighbor on the other side of the barbed wire.

"Myles!" Jake shouted and moved the UTV closer to the fence.

"How's it going?" Myles Meyer walked over.

"Good." Jake smiled. "How about yourself?"

"Busy." Myles pushed back his cowboy hat. "Did you hear about Aaron Burgess?"

"Who?" Jake feigned ignorance.

"Farmer over to the east of Shadow Bend." Myles scratched his chin. "In church this morning, they were saying he died out in his field."

"Heart attack?" Jake suggested, wanting to see what was being said.

"No one knows." Myles frowned. "But he was only in his thirties. I can't imagine it was natural causes."

"You were friends?"

Myles shook his head. "Just from church. He seemed like a nice guy though. Always willing to pitch in for the common good."

"Was he married?" Jake had almost slipped and asked about his wife until he remembered he wasn't supposed to know she existed.

"Yeah. To a local girl, but she's never around much. She's a flight attendant." Myles shrugged. "I've probably only seen her at services two or three times."

"That's got to be hard on a marriage." Jake prodded for more information.

"I'd say so." Myles nodded, then although they were the only people around, he lowered his voice. "People were saying today that they'd heard Burgess was seeing someone else."

Jake struggled to keep the intense interest out of his voice. "Any names being thrown around?"

"Nope." Myles raised his brows suggestively. "But his wife's one of the most beautiful women I've ever seen, so this other gal has to be a real looker."

CHAPTER 10
Devereaux

I came slowly awake, unsure for a moment where I was. Once I recognized my surroundings, I turned to look at the other side of the mattress. Not that I really expected Jake to be there, but I sort of hoped that just this one time he had slept in.

Still, I wasn't surprised to find his spot empty. Jake's day started before five a.m., but on Sunday, my only day off, I tended to roll out of bed closer to eight or nine.

A quick glance at the clock on the nightstand made me frown at the red numbers. What was I doing with my eyes open at seven fifteen?

Turning in early last night had obviously affected my internal snooze button. Either that or all the excitement of Mr. Burgess's death and the move had thrown me off.

One advantage of waking up now was that I could make Jake some breakfast. His habit was to do a few hours of chores before he ate, which meant he should be coming inside for some food in the next forty minutes or so.

After hopping out of bed, I quickly washed my face and tied my hair up into a messy bun. Now that I was out from under the warm covers, my legs were freezing, and I grabbed a pair of yoga pants to wear under my nightshirt.

Jake and I would have to negotiate the thermostat setting for the furnace. He preferred a chilly sixty-eight, while my body was used to Gran's seventy-four.

Hurrying into the kitchen, I turned on the oven to preheat. That should warm things up a little.

I'd probably never be as good a cook as Birdie. But ever since I'd gotten engaged, she'd been teaching me her tricks and loading my tablet with her recipes.

It had been funny to watch her figure out the device and see her type with two fingers, but she was nothing if not determined. Now that I was faced with feeding Jake and me, I appreciated her dedication.

With Ulysses, the ranch's previous chef, retired, Jake had given the hands a choice. He could hire another cook or he could give them a raise. If they chose the latter, they'd be responsible for their own meals.

I wasn't sure if I was happy or sad that they'd taken the raise. We were left with cooking for ourselves, but I didn't have to get used to some stranger using our kitchen.

This morning, I was leaning toward happy that

we no longer had a ranch cook because that left me free to attempt Gran's yummy breakfast casserole. We certainly had the eggs, fresh from the hens, and I had noticed cheddar cheese, green onion, and red bell peppers in the fridge.

Once I got the ingredients mixed and into the oven, I started the coffee and set the table. A Keurig was high on my wish list, but for now we were making do with an ancient machine that I could swear Tony had picked up at an estate sale when the last veteran of World War I died.

Don't get me wrong. I love vintage, but not where my morning cup of mental health is concerned.

I was searching the fridge for the orange juice when I heard the back door open, and I hastily grabbed the pitcher and filled the glasses that I had already put on the table.

A few seconds later, Jake walked in from the mudroom and sniffed the air. He scanned the kitchen until he spotted me, then grinned and moved toward me.

Sweeping me into his arms, he planted a kiss on my lips, then asked, "What are you doing awake so early?"

Instead of answering him, I threaded my fingers into his hair and brought his mouth back to mine. I'd foolishly fallen asleep before he made it to bed last night, and I wanted him to know that I hadn't done it intentionally.

The beeping of the stove's timer forced us apart,

and I pressed one last kiss to his lips before I wiggled out of his arms and rescued my casserole from the oven. No way was I burning our first breakfast.

"Have a seat." I motioned to the old wooden table. It had probably occupied the same spot since the house was built and badly need to be refinished, but that would have to wait until summer so I didn't end up killing myself with the fumes from the varnish. "Gran has been teaching me how to cook."

"Oh?" Jake's dark eyebrows rose as he sat in his usual chair. "When did you suddenly develop an interest in the culinary arts?"

"Well…" I drew out the word as I poured him a cup of coffee and returned the pot to its warming plate. "It was around the time she decided to entrust me with her secret recipes."

"Hmm." Jake took a sip from his mug. "Why would she do that? Didn't she say you couldn't have them until she died?"

"That was when she thought I would end up with Noah." I winked, then brought the casserole to the table and put it beside the bowl of fruit salad. Handing Jake the serving spoon, I added, "You know I only picked you so I could get the hush-hush ingredient that makes her fried chicken so good."

"Which is?" Jake helped himself to the breakfast casserole and the fruit, put his napkin in his lap, and forked a huge bite into his mouth.

Holding my hand over my heart, I shook my

head. "Sorry, I swore that I would only share it with my daughter. And then not until she got married."

"You know since we live together, I'm bound to find out." Jake continued to eat, pausing only long enough to tell me how good the casserole tasted.

Maybe I needed to hide the case of condensed cream of chicken soup that currently occupied a shelf in the pantry. He might notice that we never actually ate the soup and put two and two together.

Determined to change the subject, I asked, "What's on the agenda today?"

"I already checked the fences and creek crossings, so after breakfast, I'll finish getting the mixer wagon loaded with the feed and delivered to the pens, then I'll knock off for the day. Keel and Sam can take care of feeding the hay to the mature cow herd."

Keel and Sam being the full-time ranch hands that lived in the bunkhouse. During certain seasons, Jake employed additional help, but right now, it was just the three of them working the cattle.

"What are you planning to do with your free afternoon?" I suspected it was work our new case, but I hoped it was crawl back in bed with me.

"That chef from Lightning Bug Grill is coming out at one." Jake drained his juice glass. "After he leaves, I'd like for us to take a ride and look at the field where Burgess was found poisoned."

"That's probably a good idea." I sipped my coffee, only a little disappointed we were working rather than playing that afternoon. "It shouldn't take long to do the rest of my unpacking, then I'll try to track down Boone and Poppy. Neither one of them ever answered my text from yesterday, which is really weird."

"When you do get ahold of them, ask if they ever heard that Burgess was having an affair." Jake scraped the last bit of egg from his plate and pushed it away. "I ran into Myles Meyer over near the south pasture, and our vic was a member of his church. Meyer mentioned that Burgess's wife was rarely around and that there was speculation among the congregation that he was seeing someone else."

"Interesting." I stood up and started to clear the table. "That would certainly provide a motive if his death proves to be murder."

Jake brought his plate, silverware, and juice glass to the dishwasher and placed them inside. Thankfully, his aunt had installed the appliance when she'd remodeled the old kitchen, because, while I was beginning to enjoy cooking, I hated the washing up.

After kissing me, Jake headed toward the back door, but before he left, he paused and said, "If you get time, why don't you do an internet search on Burgess and his wife. Check out social media and see if you can catch any hints that their marriage was rocky. Also, print out pictures of them both."

"Will do." I saluted because he was my boss when I was wearing my private detective hat.

Once I had cleaned up the kitchen and started the

dishwasher, I returned to the bedroom and put away the few things that I had yet to unpack. Then I made the bed, tidied up the bathroom, and headed to Jake's office.

We had gotten rid of the old writing table that Tony had used for the past fifty years and moved in an elegant burled walnut partners' desk that I found on a local auction site. I dropped into the chair on my side and booted up the desktop.

While I waited for the computer to come to life, I checked my phone again. It was a relief to see a text from Poppy, but Boone was still radio silent.

Poppy's message was short but informative.

AARON BURGESS IS A CUSTOMER. HE'S A NICE GUY. NO RUMORS ABOUT HIM. CALL WHEN YOU HAVE A CHANCE. HOW WAS THE MOVE-IN SEX WITH JAKE?

She had added a smirking emoji and I laughed. Wouldn't she be disappointed to know that we'd both fallen asleep instead of having sexy times?

It was early for Poppy to be up. Her bar didn't close until two on Saturday nights. I wondered if she'd sent the text before going to bed and it hadn't been delivered until now. Our cell service wasn't the best out here.

Just in case she was still sleeping, I decided to wait to call her until after ten. However, since I hadn't heard from Boone, I did try him, but his phone went straight to voicemail.

I left a message asking that he call me ASAP, then

got to work searching for Rose and Aaron Burgess's social media accounts. It was shocking how much people revealed about themselves on those sites, and as private investigators, Jake and I took full advantage of their naïveté.

CHAPTER 11
Devereaux

I resisted calling to see how Birdie and Tony were doing. Beckham Janson had agreed to update Jake and me via text every day at noon and then again at ten. And if there was an emergency, he had all our phone numbers. This included both our cells, as well as the landlines at the house, dime store, and Jake's office.

Hmm! Maybe I should add Dad's cell phone and the one at Catherine's art gallery just to be on the safe side.

Even though last night's message had been reassuring, I still worried about Gran. In the past fourteen years, we'd rarely spent a night apart.

Beckham's ten o'clock text had stated that, as planned, he'd arrived at five, settled into my old room, and had dinner with Gran and Tony. Then the three of them had watched *Dark Passage*, a Humphry Bogart and Lauren Bacall movie. After ice cream and the early news, they were all going to bed.

I also refrained from phoning my father to see if

his stint managing the dime store had gone okay. In my head, I knew he would have gotten in touch with me if there was a problem, but in my heart, I still wanted the reassurance of knowing that nothing had happened to my business in my absence.

Fortunately, Aaron's and Rose's social media accounts were interesting enough to keep my attention and stop me from checking up on my family. Both of them were addicted to selfies. Aaron's showed a mildly attractive guy in his late twenties or early thirties with closely cropped dark hair, whiskey-colored eyes, and a lanky build.

His photo history was mostly snapshots of him and his buddies dressed in uniforms and leaning against tanks and Humvees. More current pictures were of him in jeans and a flannel shirt working around the farm or drinking beer with a group of guys in Gossip Central.

It was interesting to note that all his buddies were wearing caps advertising John Deer and Pioneer Seeds. This led me to believe that he mostly hung out with other local farmers. The ranchers would have had on cowboy hats, and the white-collar dudes around here were generally bareheaded.

Rose's social media photos were of exotic locations or glam shots. She was a stunningly beautiful woman with a cloud of rich espresso-brown hair surrounding her exquisite face and luminous light blue eyes. Her photos were mesmerizing, and although it was superficial of me, I couldn't imagine what in the heck she was doing married to a farmer in Podunk, Missouri.

Still, I didn't see any pictures or references to her with other men or him with other women. Then again, there were also very few photos of them together. Did that mean anything?

I printed out the headshots that Jake had requested, typed a summary of what I'd seen on social media about Rose and Aaron, and turned off the computer.

It was a few minutes past ten, so I grabbed my phone and dialed Poppy's number. As it rang, I headed into the master bath.

My plan was to use our chat time to put on some makeup, fix my hair, and get dressed. I wanted to meet the Lightning Bug Grill chef, and I didn't want the man to think Jake was engaged to one of Cinderella's ugly stepsisters.

On the fifth ring, Poppy said, "How's the test marriage going?"

"Busy."

"I bet," she snickered.

"Sadly, not in that way." I retrieved my makeup case from the vanity drawer and leaned closer to the mirror. "Noah managed to divert our attention."

"What!" Poppy's screech almost burst my eardrum, and I quickly swiped the speaker icon, then put my cell phone on the counter.

After explaining the situation, up to and

including my visit to the sheriff's office, I said, "Which is why I wanted to talk to you about Aaron Burgess."

"You mean the poor guy is dead and no one knows what happened?"

"Pretty much." I dusted on some bronzer. With my pale complexion, I looked like a ghost if I didn't add some artificial color. "Your text said that you haven't heard any gossip about him, right?"

"None at all." Poppy sighed. "He usually comes in a couple of nights a week, sits at the bar, and shoots the breeze with his farmer pals."

"Is he a heavy drinker?"

I patted concealer under my eyes. Even when I was fully rested, I still had dark circles. Another hassle of having fair skin.

"Nope. I'll never get rich off of his bar tab." Poppy blew out a breath. "He has maybe three beers at the most."

"Is his wife ever with him?" I brushed on some peachy-pink eyeshadow. "Or any other women?"

"I've seen Rose with him on a couple of occasions, but never anyone else." Poppy paused, then added, "You know about her, right?"

"No. What about her?" I coated my lashes with mascara.

Had I missed something on social media? I'd only gone back a year or so.

"Rose left Shadow Bend right after high school and headed to New York to be a model." There was something in Poppy's voice that I'd never heard before. Could it be jealousy? "The first three or four years, she was doing really well. She'd gotten on with a famous agency, was on the cover of lots of important magazines, and on the runway for all the top designers during fashion week."

"Wow." Now for my hair. If I wanted to do anything with it, I had to either put it in hot curlers or get out my straightener. Which did I feel like messing with today? I decided on the flat iron, plugged it in, and asked, "How did she end up back here?"

Poppy's tone changed from envious to disgusted. "Because of the stupid paparazzi's starting ugly rumors about her."

"What kind of rumors?" I hated it when my BFF made me beg for each tidbit of information.

"She was dating an up-and-coming sports star who turned out to have a wife and kids stashed away at home that no one knew about." Poppy tsked, "The tabloids splashed Rose's face across all those supermarket rags accusing her of being a homewrecker."

"Of course, it was her fault, not the guy's." I rolled my eyes as I clipped my hair into six sections.

"He did an interview with some big entertainment host and claimed that he'd told Rose that he was married and she'd seduced him anyway." Poppy snorted. "I'm sure his team's PR firm arranged the whole thing and put out the word Rose had only gone after this guy to get more publicity for her modeling career."

Running the flat iron over small pieces of my hair, I worked my way through all the loose segments as I asked, "Did Rose's agency drop her?"

"No one knows exactly what happened." Poppy chuckled. "Not that the Shadow Bend gossips didn't try to find out, but Rose just vanished."

"Wow." The bottom half of my hair was now nice and sleek, so I let down the top half and started on it. "No one knew where she was?"

"Her mom was already dead, and her father might have known Rose's whereabouts, but he wasn't talking."

"That was smart of him." I finished up my hair and admired the smooth fall from my crown to the middle of my back. "When did Rose return to Shadow Bend?"

"About a year or so after the scandal broke, her dad had a stroke. She came back here to take care of him." Poppy's voice cracked. "He didn't last much longer, but at least she had a few months with him."

"Let's see." While I mentally figured out the chronology, I picked up my cell phone and moved into the bedroom to change clothes. "If Rose left at eighteen and she's twenty-seven now, she must have been a freshman when you and I were seniors."

"That's right," Poppy agreed. "I remember she was on the junior varsity cheerleading squad when I was on the varsity squad."

"When did she marry Aaron?" I selected a pair of black jeans and a light gray roll-neck sweater.

"It was shortly after her father passed away. Aaron had been helping out with Mr. Chagall's land because it was next to the Burgess farm."

"Which means Rose and Aaron probably were childhood friends." I pulled on short black boots and walked over to the mirror. "I wonder if they dated before she left for New York and he went into the army."

"I could find out," Poppy offered.

"Maybe later." I flipped open my jewelry box and selected a pair of silver earrings. "Were there any rumors about Aaron and Rose's marriage?"

"Not that I heard." Poppy paused. "I do remember that right before they got engaged, there was some incident where a guy was paying her too much attention and his girlfriend revived the old gossip about Rose's relationship with that sports star. But once Rose and Aaron were married, all the talk died down again."

"Interesting." I slipped a long silver chain over my head and adjusted it under my collar. "Hey, before I hang up, have you heard from Boone yesterday or today?"

"No!" Poppy's voice rose. "I meant to ask you about him first thing, but you distracted me with Aaron's murder. Boone hasn't answered his phone since Friday afternoon. Do you think we should contact his parents and see if he's okay?"

I thought it over, then said, "Let's wait until tonight. "If we don't hear from him before ten, we probably should give them a call." Frowning, I added, "What could he be doing that he's not even checking his phone?"

"I hope it's because he met someone and is so busy in bed he's not even thinking about the outside world."

My chest tightened. "Fingers crossed."

I didn't have a good feeling about Boone's silence. He hadn't mentioned dating anyone new in a long time. That, along with his recent unavailability whenever I suggested that the three of us have a movie night or go to dinner or hang out together, made me suspect that he might be depressed.

Maybe while Jake was busy with the chef, I should pop over to Boone's place and check things out. I could see if his car was in the garage or if there were lights on in the house or if I could hear anything.

I had Boone's key for emergencies and to feed his cat, Tsar, when he was out of town. I just had to decide if this was a crisis or if Poppy and I were just being mother hens.

<u>CHAPTER 12</u>
Devereaux

After Poppy and I said our goodbyes, I went into the kitchen to make a fresh pot of French roast for the Lightning Bug chef. Luckily, there was plenty of Gran's black walnut tart left so I could offer him something with his coffee. Otherwise, his options would be a package of some generic chocolate chip cookies that had been residing in the pantry as long as I could remember.

Note to self: Throw out the cookies and get some pastries from the Shadow Bend bakery to put in the deep freeze for emergencies. I already had a standing requisition for the dime store's craft group get-togethers, and I could just add a couple dozen more to take home.

While I contemplated which baked goods to add to my order, I got out cups, plates, napkins, and silverware. By the time the back door slammed and Jake strode through the mudroom and into the kitchen, the table was set and I was answering e-mail on my phone.

A ripe aroma preceded Jake like a wave of dung perfume, and I was glad he didn't stop for a kiss as he moved through the room. But by the scowl on his handsome face, I was pretty sure romance was the last thing on his mind.

He was already unbuttoning his shirt when he called over his shoulder, "This morning Tank seems to have explosive diarrhea and impeccable aim, so I need to catch a quick shower. Can you keep an eye out for Chef Niall?"

Tank was Jake's prize bull. For such a large animal, he had a very delicate stomach. If there was one petal of something like cypress leaf in the whole pasture, he'd find it, eat it, and expel it in the most noxious manner possible.

"Sure," I yelled to Jake's retreating figure as he disappeared into our bedroom. "Do you want to meet with the chef in the kitchen? I have refreshments ready."

Jake's voice drifted back to me. "Good idea."

A few minutes later, the doorbell rang and I hurried into the foyer. I might be a country girl, but I'd had enough big-city experience to look through the side window before I turned the deadbolt.

When Jake had mentioned that Cameron Niall was coming out to discuss purchasing some of the Del Vecchio beef, I'd Googled the chef. The man standing on our porch was definitely him. A slightly older version but him. This guy's brown hair had some gray, as did his Van Dyke beard and mustache, but he was still recognizable.

Opening the door, I said, "Hi. I'm Devereaux Sinclair, Jake's fiancée."

"Cam Niall." He shook my hand. "Chef owner of the Lightning Bug Grill."

"Please come inside. Jake will join us in a minute." I motioned for him to follow me and led him to the kitchen. "Have a seat. Would you like coffee?"

"That'd be great." Cam smiled and sat down.

I poured him a cup, then asked, "Cream? Sugar?"

"Black is fine." He lifted a brow. "As long as it's the good stuff."

I made a noncommittal face and crossed my fingers that the beans I'd chosen were up to snuff. I was pretty picky and I liked them, but this guy had a trained palate.

Figuring I might as well go all in, I motioned to the cake stand in the center of the table and said, "That's my Gran's blue-ribbon-winning black walnut and caramel tart. Would you like a slice?"

"How can I resist after a buildup like that?" The chef grinned and asked, "Does your grandmother live with you?"

"No." I sliced into the tart. "She just provides us with desserts because I'm not much of a baker."

"I'm sure you have other good qualities to make up for your lack of culinary skills," Cam flirted.

I made a noncommittal noise and passed him a

piece of the tart. As he accepted the plate, Jake marched into the room and introduced himself. He took a seat opposite the chef and asked him about his drive down from Kansas City.

While the men chatted, I poured two more cups of coffee, put one in front of Jake, and kept the other as I sat next to him.

After twenty minutes of product discussion, Cam finished Gran's tart and sent her his compliments, then requested a tour of the ranch. We all stood up, and the chef walked into the hallway.

I pulled Jake aside before he could follow him and said, "I'm worried about Boone. He hasn't answered any of my texts, and Poppy hasn't been able to get in touch with him either."

Jake's forehead wrinkled. "That is odd." He was well aware of how close I was to my two BFFs.

"While you show Cam around, I'll zip into town and check out Boone's place." As I headed into the bedroom to get my purse, I called over my shoulder, "I should be back in less than an hour."

"Let me know if you need me." Jake blew me a kiss, then hurried to join the chef.

Once I found my purse and left the bedroom, the men were long gone, so I locked up the house and jumped into my sapphire black Z4. It was one of the few possessions that I had kept from my old life—the one where I earned a six-figure salary as an investment consultant employed by Stramp

Investments.

I'd sold off most of the nice things that I owned. The designer purses, shoes, and suits had all gone to consignment shops, and I'd peddled my jewelry on eBay, but I had allowed myself to hang on to the BMW by rationalizing that I'd never get what it was worth if I sold it.

However, the truth was that I loved that car, and I knew in my current financial circumstances there was more chance of me winning the lottery than ever owning a vehicle like it again.

Chuckling at the thought of hitting the Mega Millions, considering that I'd never bought a single ticket, I put the Z4 in gear and headed to Boone's. He lived in the old-money part of town. His neighborhood was full of stately hundred-year or older residences with manicured lawns and perfectly pruned trees.

Because his parents had made it clear to Boone's grandmother that they preferred the contemporary home they'd built a few streets over, she had left him her prairie-style house. She knew that Boone loved the place and would lavish it with his cash and attention.

Which he had, keeping the original structure intact while enlarging and remodeling the master bathroom, converting one of the four upstairs bedrooms into a walk-in closet, and adding a detached garage in the rear of the property.

When a few folks from the historical society had questioned his renovations, Boone had informed then that while vintage was wonderful, there was no need to go overboard in the quest for authenticity. After all, he liked reading Jane Austen, but he had no desire to live in England's Regency period, where people reused tea leaves and wore jewelry made from their dead mother's hair.

I parked in Boone's empty driveway. I was never comfortable when I was forced to leave my Z4 on the street, vulnerable to all the idiot drivers just waiting to sideswipe it. I had minimal auto insurance and a sky-high deductible, which meant I'd never be able to afford to have the car repaired if it got dented. And call me shallow, but it would kill me to drive around in a less than pristine vehicle.

Getting out of my BMW, I headed toward the garage. Peering inside, I could see that Boone's Mercedes was there. If he wasn't home, someone had picked him up.

As I returned to the front of the house and walked up to the door, I admired the grouping of multipaned windows that were the focal point of the second floor. No matter how many times I saw them, they always drew my attention and made me smile.

I rang the bell, and after a few minutes when there was no answer, I jabbed the button several more times. Then I tried both his landline and cell number again, but like all my previous attempts to call him, I was immediately shunted to voicemail.

Either Boone wasn't home or something had

happened to him. The question was, should I use my key or not?

CHAPTER 13
Devereaux

Before I began the arduous task of digging through my purse to locate Boone's key in its cavernous depths, I called Poppy. Gossip Central opened at noon on Sunday, so I knew that she'd be working, but I was fairly certain that the bar wouldn't be too busy.

This time of year, the place was usually pretty quiet until later in the afternoon when the Cardinals or Royals game came on TV. With Shadow Bend being closer to Kansas City than St. Louis, the townspeople's loyalty shouldn't have been divided between the two teams, but there were enough transplants and rebels to make things interesting.

Most people chose a side and only tuned in to games that featured their favored team. Personally, I couldn't understand why the sports enthusiasts couldn't watch both.

And don't get me started about the ridiculous

fights that erupted when the Cards played the Royals. It was almost as amusing as when the Cubs played the White Sox and entire families were divided.

My thoughts about silly rivalries were interrupted when Poppy picked up on the third ring and demanded, "Did you find Boone?"

"No. I'm at his house and his car is here but he isn't answering the doorbell." Anticipating her questions, I explained my movements thus far, then asked, "Do you think I should use my key?"

"Duh!" Poppy's bellow nearly burst my eardrum. "Why else are you there?"

Invading anyone's privacy, even someone with whom I'd been friends since childhood, struck me as wrong and I stalled, "Maybe we should check with his parents first."

Poppy blew out an annoyed raspberry. "Would you want me to call Birdie if I couldn't get in touch with you and was worried? Or, since we're all adults, would you want me to check your house first?"

"Good point."

Having crossed the thirty-year-old mark, none of us would want to involve our family unless things were really bad. And now that I had finally moved out and was living on my own, I could understand even better how Poppy or Boone might feel about their folks being alerted to their absence before it was clear whether or not there was a real problem.

"Look." Poppy's voice dragged me back to the matter at hand. "You'll find one of three things. He's not there. He's there, but he's sick or injured. He's found someone and is too busy in bed to answer his phone or hear you ringing his doorbell and knocking."

"True," I reluctantly agreed, not entirely convinced by her argument and still unwilling to barge into my friend's house uninvited. It made me feel like a busybody. "Even so—"

Poppy interrupted me, "Listen to me and just do it. How can you stand there picturing poor Boone in some horrible mess?"

"My lack of imagination is my only defense against immobilizing myself with imaginary fears," I retorted.

"Stop being such a dipstick." Poppy was clearly not amused by my quip. "If Boone's not home, no harm, no foul. If he's sick or injured. You might save his life and he'll be grateful for the help."

"And if it's the third option you mentioned?" I snapped, irritated because I knew she was correct.

"It will be momentarily embarrassing." Poppy giggled. "But oh, so much fun to tease him about in the years ahead. And it will serve him right for being so darned secretive about his relationships."

"Fine." During our drawn-out conversation, I had located Boone's key, and now I stuck it in the lock. "I'll let you know what happens."

Disconnecting from Poppy, I kept the phone in my hand. I didn't want to have to fumble for it if I needed to summon help right away.

The door swung open silently on well-oiled hinges, and I stepped inside, calling, "Boone? It's Dev. Sorry to burst in on you. I'm just checking to make sure everything's all right because you're not answering my calls or texts. Are you okay?"

There was no answer, and I carefully examined the front hallway. It looked the same as it usually did when I visited Boone. Polished wood floors, taupe walls, and a small mission-style oak table under a mirror.

The Roseville pottery clematis-blue bowl on the tabletop was empty. When Boone was at home, it usually contained his keys and wallet. I took that as a good sign. Or at least a sign that he wasn't lying somewhere with a broken neck or passed out from some debilitating illness. That is, unless he'd been robbed.

However, the house felt empty, and I didn't see anything that suggested forced entry. I peered into the parlor. Nothing was disturbed in there, and the oak curio cabinet that held Boone's collection of valuable miniature sculptures appeared undisturbed.

Biting my lip, I made my way into the kitchen. The four wooden slat-back chairs were precisely pulled up to the matching square-leg table. The sink was empty and there wasn't anything on the counters.

Which wasn't surprising. Boone was a bit of a neat freak. If there were dirty dishes or crumbs, I would have been concerned.

While I moved throughout the remaining rooms

on the ground floor, I kept announcing my presence. But I could have saved my breath. There didn't seem to be anyone around to hear my shouts.

I kept the library for last. This was my favorite spot in Boone's house and the one he hung out in the most. Its large windows were framed in whiskey-colored draperies that were artfully pooled on the shiny hardwood floor. A hexagon Limbert side table holding a vintage cut glass wedge vase with a charming arrangement of sweet peas, snapdragons, and peonies was positioned behind a nutmeg leather sofa. The finishing touch was an assortment of brass lamps that were scattered throughout the space.

I had hoped to find Boone sitting in one of the matching club chairs, so engrossed in some legal tome that he was oblivious to my shouts, but sadly, that wasn't the case. This room, like all the others that I had explored, was unoccupied.

Which only left the three bedrooms upstairs.

In my heart of hearts, I knew that if I was going to find something either dreadful or embarrassing, those were the most likely places.

I slowly climbed the steps, yoohooing after each one. At the landing, I stopped to see if I could hear anything, but there wasn't even the ticking of Boone's grandfather clock to break the silence. It had stopped working last week, and he hadn't been able to find anyone willing to travel to Shadow Bend to repair it.

Giving in to my sense of dread, I checked the two

guest rooms first. When I found them unoccupied, I forced myself to approach the master suite.

The door was ajar, and I held my breath as I pushed it open with the tip of my finger. A quick glance at the spacious room assured me that Boone wasn't there.

I'd only been in this room once or twice, but as far as I could tell, it looked the same. The bed was made, the drawers were shut, and the area rugs were in place.

That left the attached master bath. Much to my relief, it too was empty.

However, I did detect a clue when I caught the aroma of Boone's aftershave lingering in the air. It was Gentlemen Only by Givenchy, the one he saved for important dates.

The last time he was here, he was definitely getting ready to go out with someone special. Judging by the faintness of the scent and Boone's penchant for a heavy hand when spraying it on himself, it had to have been at least a day or so ago since he'd applied it.

Feeling somewhat relieved, I called Poppy. When she answered, I reported my findings.

There was a slight pause, then Poppy said, "So you think he had a hot tryst Saturday night and he's still with her?"

"Yes." I bit my lip. "The one weird thing is that he didn't take his car."

"Yeah. Boone loves that Mercedes and he likes to show it off."

"Exactly." I made my way downstairs. "I'm going to check the garage again."

"Good idea." Poppy's agreement was terse, and I could tell she was worried.

Luckily the set of keys that Boone had given me had one that was to the garage's pedestrian door, because I didn't want to try to lift the other one. I didn't have clue as to why he didn't have an automatic opener, but having been the designated hoister on several occasions, I knew how heavy it was.

I stepped inside, found the light switch, and flicked it upward. Along the walls were various tools, a lawn mower, and a bike, but Boone's Mercedes shined in solitary splendor in the center of the cement floor.

Approaching it, I peered through the driver's window, then reported to Poppy, "There's nothing in the car."

"Hmm."

I hadn't noticed before, but when I glanced down, I squealed, "Yikes!"

"What?" Poppy yelped in my ear. "Is it Boone?"

"Nope. It's his tires. All four have been slashed."

"That does it. I'm calling my dad." There was a tremor in Poppy's voice.

"Probably a good idea." Something had just occurred to me. "Because not only is Boone MIA, so is his Tsar."

"The cat is missing too?" Poppy squealed. "That

can't be good."

"No, it can't." My heart was racing. "He loves that Russian Blue almost as much as he does us. Grabbing Tsar would be a good way of controlling Boone."

CHAPTER 14
Jake

Jake continued to listen with half an ear as Niall rhapsodized about the beef that he was ordering from the Del Vecchio Ranch. The chef had wanted to see everything, and their tour of the operation via the UTV had been a lot more in-depth than Jake had estimated.

The expedition had taken forever, and they'd only gotten back to the house a few minutes ago. Niall had examined all three livestock barns, the utility and storage buildings, the equipment and tool sheds, and the pastures. Jake sighed. The guy had even wanted to see the bunkhouse.

As they finally reentered the kitchen, Jake felt his cell vibrate. Although he was anxiously waiting for Devereaux to contact him about her findings at Boone's house, he made himself ignore the alert.

However, as soon as the chef excused himself to

use the can, Jake pulled out his phone. He frowned as he read Devereaux's text that Boone was missing.

First there was a mysterious poisoning and now this. What was going on in Shadow Bend?

Hearing the toilet flush, Jake quickly typed a reply. I'M STILL WITH THE CLIENT. DO YOU WANT ME TO MEET YOU AT BOONE'S?

He stared at the screen, but when there was no immediate answer, he slipped the device into his pocket and hurried to his office to grab the contract. He got back to the kitchen just as Niall entered from the guest bath off the hallway.

The chef took a seat, and Jake slid the document across the tabletop to him. "This is our standard agreement. If it looks okay to you, you can fill in the quantity you want to purchase, the frequency of the delivery, and the price that we've discussed."

"Give me a minute," Niall muttered as he took out a pen and made entries on the contract. A few minutes later, he glanced up and scowled, "No credit?"

"Sorry." Jake shook his head. "We'll expect a check when the meat is delivered."

"Then you'll need to call ahead to give us the final dollar amount," Niall cautioned, then when Jake nodded, he signed the contract with a flourish.

Jake took the document, added his signature, and said, "Come with me to my office and I'll make you a copy, then walk you to your car."

Jake stood and waited impatiently for the chef to

follow suit. Once the man got to his feet, Jake strode quickly down the hall, glancing over his shoulder to make sure Niall was keeping up with him. He wanted to get rid of this guy ASAP so he'd be available if Devereaux needed him.

Fifteen minutes later, the chef's Land Rover disappeared down the driveway in a cloud of dust. An instant later, Jake had his cell in his hand and was reading Devereaux's most recent message.

CHIEF KINCAID SAID THERE'S NOTHING HE CAN DO BECAUSE BOONE HASN'T BEEN MISSING LONG ENOUGH. I'LL HEAD BACK TO THE RANCH IN A FEW MINUTES. I SHOULD BE THERE BY FOUR. POPPY IS PISSED!

Jake checked the time. It was three forty-eight.

He turned on his heel to go inside the house and clean up the cups and plates that he and the chef had used, but as he put his hand on the doorknob, he heard a car coming down the lane. It didn't sound like Devereaux's BMW, so he paused to see who was approaching the ranch.

A few seconds later, he scowled when he recognized the bright green Charger racing toward him. Until recently it had resided in a storage unit in St. Louis but had appeared in Shadow Bend about a month ago. What in blue blazes was his ex-wife doing here?

Meg had always been a terror on the road. None of her partners had been willing to ride with her when she'd been a marshal, but even for her, the speed she was taking the rutted gravel lane was a bit much. Something was wrong.

Jake debated stepping into the safety of the house's interior, but before he could take action, the Charger slid to a stop. A nanosecond later, Meg hopped out of the Dodge and sauntered up the steps and onto the porch.

From her tight leather pants and jacket to the midriff-revealing top, she was dressed entirely in black. Her scarlet lipstick was a stark contrast to her monochromatically dark attire.

"Why are you here?" Jake blocked her from advancing any farther.

Meg widened her forest-green eyes. "Is this how you greet your wife?"

"Ex," Jake gritted. They'd been divorced longer than they'd been married, yet she played this game every time he saw her. "What do you want?"

She must have noticed him gazing down the driveway, and her mouth curled into a sly smile. "Ah. Are you expecting someone soon?"

"Either tell me what's going on or leave." Jake ignored her question.

Meg ran her fingers over his chest, and he swatted her hand away.

Pouting, she said, "Don't be like that. Remember all the good times we had?"

"No." He crossed his arms. "What kind of game are you playing now?"

One of the many problems with his ex was her utter conviction that she deserved whatever she could grab away from someone else. Another was that she was more of a con artist than the criminals they pursued. He could smell one of her scams from a mile away.

"Fine. Be that way." Meg pursed her lips and blew out an annoyed breath. Every cell of her body emitted irritability that he wasn't falling all over himself to do whatever she wanted. "You're going to find something out when you start investigating Aaron Burgess, and I need you to keep your mouth shut about it."

Jake wrinkled his brow, his mind racing with the little he knew about the man. What secret was she talking about, and why would she care?

An instant later, he pointed a finger at her and said, "You were cheating on Underwood with Burgess."

"I never promised Noah that we'd be exclusive." Meg frowned, the line between her eyebrows more pronounced than it had been a year ago. "He just sort of assumed it, and I never bothered to correct him."

"Because you liked him not seeing anyone else." Jake chuckled. "Same old Meg."

"Yep." She shrugged. "Aaron and I both had a good reason to keep the affair on the down low. He loved his wife, and I loved the money Noah spent on me."

"So why was Burgess screwing you if he loved Rose?" Jake raised a brow.

"She has issues in the bedroom. Something that happened to her in the past." Meg shrugged again. "I didn't ask for details, because frankly, I didn't care." She swallowed, then shook her head. "We all have had to deal with trauma. Survival of the fittest and all that crap."

"Seriously?" Jake was sympathetic about his ex's experience at the hands of a deranged serial killer, but clearly Meg didn't extend the same empathy to others. "You have no compassion for the woman?"

"You don't have to bite off my head." She waved her hand as if shooing away a mosquito.

"Right." Jake rolled his eyes. "Why bother when a reptile like you regenerates?"

"Whatever." Meg seemed immune to his insult. "Anyway, Aaron and I would meet up when the missus was off flying, do the nasty, get it out of our system, then pretend we never knew each other."

"How in hades did you keep it a secret?" Jake would have bet money that kind of thing would be headline news in Shadow Bend.

"We met at the Sleep on Inn near the highway and made it a point to arrive separately and leave separately." Meg stuck her hands in her jacket pockets. "But I know once you start poking around and showing his picture to people, one of the employees at the motel will recognize Aaron and then describe me." She smiled crookedly. "After all, you were the second-best marshal in the organization."

He had been the best, but Jake didn't bother to argue. He couldn't think of any reason to spill the beans to the doc. Meg's cheating on the man wasn't any skin off Jake's nose, and keeping her involved with Underwood meant that she was out of Jake's hair.

"Well," Jake drew out the word just enough to make Meg anxious, then twitched his shoulders. "Unless I find out you had something to do with Burgess's death, I won't include your name in my report to the good doctor."

"I knew I could count on you." Meg fluffed her hair and turned to leave.

An instant later, she whirled around, threw her arms around Jake's neck, and attempted to kiss him.

He was shoving her away when he heard a car door slam and a gasp. How had he missed Devereaux pulling into the driveway?

CHAPTER 15
Devereaux

Well! That hadn't been what I expected to see when I got home.

It only took me a second to assess the situation. Meg's arms were wound around Jake's neck, and he had a hold of her shoulders. However, by the disgusted expression on his face and the way he was shoving her away, he certainly didn't look like a cooperating party.

Because of my previous experience with untrustworthy men, my first instinct was to think that Jake's attempt to fend off his ex was for my benefit. But once I pushed my distrust aside and took in a few more details, it was clear that Meg was attempting to stage a scene that would upset me.

Jake was pressed against the front door as if he'd backed as far away from her as he could get. Then there was the fact that he knew that I was due home any minute. Even if I was willing to believe he was a cheat, there was no way that he was that stupid.

The clincher was when Meg turned her head and shot me a triumphant smile. As I suspected, the witch had set up Jake.

Aside from being the most manipulative woman I had ever met, which was quite the accomplishment considering what Noah's mother had put me through, I just couldn't understand what she thought she would accomplish by doing something like that.

Even if Jake and I didn't get married, there was no way in hell that he'd ever take her back. Maybe she couldn't stand to see him happy. Or she just hated me. Or she was the epitome of evil.

Probably that last one.

Okay. That was a bit nasty. But Meg drew meanness out of me as if I were made of steel and she was a magnet.

Refusing to fall into her trap, I waved cheerily and called out, "Honey, I'm home."

The relief on Jake's face was hilarious. With a mighty heave ho, he propelled Meg aside with such force she teetered on the high heels of her trampy boots. Either he didn't notice that she was about to take a tumble or didn't care, because he ignored his ex and dashed down the porch steps toward me as if the hounds of hell were after him and he was their favorite chew toy.

Jake swept me into his arms, and just before his lips landed on mine, he muttered, "That was not what it looks like."

Once he had thoroughly kissed me and I regained my breath, I chuckled. "Of course not. But I can't wait to hear the story behind it."

In the meantime, Meg had regained her balance or gotten back to her feet—I had been too busy making out with my fiancé to notice if she'd actually fallen or not. But now she sauntered to her car, *accidently* digging into my back with her elbow as she passed us.

Getting into the bright green Dodge, she raised her voice and called out, "Sugar britches, don't forget your promise to keep our little secret."

Apparently confident of his answer, she wiggled her fingers out the window and drove off.

"I see we both had some excitement," I teased as I leaned back in Jake's arms and looked him in the eye.

"Any news on Boone?" Jake took my hand, led me to the porch swing, and sat down.

"Nope. I left a note taped to his front door, and Poppy is bound and determined to hack his phone's tracking app." I attempted to sit next to Jake, but he pulled me onto his lap. The chain holding the swing groaned and I held my breath. "Since I'm not exactly a lightweight and your muscles are pretty heavy too, maybe we should reinforce this thing before we start canoodling out here."

"Canoodle?" Jake tightened his hold as I tried to stand up. "Where did you get that word from?"

"I guess I've been hanging around Birdie too long." Giggling, I added, "Do you think she and your uncle are doing their own canoodling right now?"

"If they are, more power to them." Jake nuzzled my neck. "And the swing is fine. I remember Tony and my aunt out here when I was a boy, and neither one of them was skinny."

"Hmm." I wasn't convinced, but I was enjoying his kisses, and I figured we didn't have too far to fall if he was wrong.

"Does Chief Kincaid know what Poppy's up to?" Jake asked.

"He probably has a good idea." I sighed. "She closed Gossip Central to come into town and talk to him about Boone's absence, and she never closes that place. He had to know that she would be upset when he said there wasn't anything the police could do."

"Shoot!" Jake shook his head. "I sure hope they don't have another falling-out over this."

"Me too."

Poppy and her dad had been at odds for a long time and only recently resolved most of their issues. I could definitely see this causing some problems with their relationship. Both of them were stubborn as a toddler demanding a toy at the grocery store checkout counter.

After a little more cuddling, Jake asked, "Are you up for some investigating? I need to visit the field where Burgess was working. I'm hoping the sheriff's department won't have been out there yet, because I'd like to get a look before they get around to marking it a crime scene."

"Sure. Poppy will text me if she hears anything."
I jumped to my feet. "But let me grab an apple or
something to eat on the way. I didn't get any lunch,
did you?"

"I had a sandwich with the hands before Chef
Niall arrived." Jake stood. "You go ahead and fetch
your snack while I put your car in the garage and pull
the truck up.

After tossing him my keys, I ran into the house.
While I was there, I used the bathroom, then stuffed
an apple and a granola bar into my jacket pocket.

Jake was waiting when I walked out the front
door. I quickly hopped into the passenger seat, and as
he drove down the driveway, I took a bite of the
Granny Smith. I loved the tartness of that variety, and
I usually chose it over the more popular Red
Delicious.

Once I'd satisfied my hunger, I said, "What's the
story with Meg?"

"Do you promise to keep this between you and
me?" Jake slid a glance in my direction.

"Okay." I hoped I wasn't being too hasty in
agreeing to his terms.

Jake made the turn to head east of town.
"Remember this morning at breakfast when I
mentioned that there was a rumor floating around that
Burgess had an affair?"

"Sure. I didn't get a chance to ask Poppy about it,
and of course, with Boone MIA, I haven't been able to

pick his brain yet either." As I answered Jake's question, the reason for his query popped into my mind, and I squealed, "You've got to be kidding me! Are you saying that Meg…?"

"Yep." Jake's expression was anything but shocked. "She was messing around with Burgess behind Underwood's back."

"That woman needs to leave Shadow Bend before someone drops a house on her," I huffed. "And when they do, I'm grabbing her ruby slippers."

Jake chuckled. "You seem stunned."

"You weren't?"

"Nothing Meg does could surprise me." Jake tapped his fingers on the steering wheel. "Although, I was astounded that she and Burgess were able to keep it a secret."

"But did they?" I bit my lip. "We really need to check the wife's alibi."

"And Underwood's."

"If Noah was behind it, would he really hire you to investigate?"

"He's a smart man." Jake's tone was grudging. "What better way to avoid suspicion than be the one who demands an investigation?"

"I don't think Noah cares that much about Meg." I was still convinced that he really loved Poppy but, for some obscure reason, wouldn't admit it to himself. "There's not a lot of chemistry or even affection between them. At least not that I've been able to observe."

"We really haven't seen them together much." Jake slowed the truck.

"Then I guess we'll have to take him up on that double date offer." I watched as Jake eased the Ford into a pull off leading into a field.

"Let's try a few other investigative methods first." Jake turned his head and stared at me. "But in the meantime, no blabbing to Poppy or Boone, and especially to Underwood, about Meg and Burgess's affair."

"I'll keep my promise," I pouted, then narrowed my eyes and added, "But once the case is solved, Noah needs to hear the truth."

CHAPTER 16
Devereaux

"What I don't understand is why would Meg kiss
you in front of me, when she knows that would make
you mad? If she needs you to keep her secret, why go
out of her way to antagonize you?"

Jake and I were examining the area where Aaron
had been found unconscious. We knew we were in the
right place because an old tractor, one like my
grandfather used to drive, was still sitting in the field.
Quito had mentioned that Aaron loved the antique
Farmall and often used it instead of one of the newer
models they owned.

"Meg thinks the world revolves around her and
that she is smarter than everyone else." Jake paused
and pointed to the ground. "The grass here is packed
down. I'll bet this is where they had lunch."

As I studied the area Jake indicated, then
dropped to my knees and started slowly running my
fingers through the unmatted grass around that spot, I

continued my musings, "Still, Meg has to realize that after what she did to you, it's risky to annoy you when she needs a favor."

"Who knows what that woman thinks," he muttered as he walked away and entered the field.

Jake didn't seem all that interested in discussing his ex's motives or reasoning, but I knew that familiar enemies were the easiest to defeat. Which was why I wanted to understand Meg. Not as much as I wanted her to move back to St. Louis, but close.

With half my mind still trying to figure out Meg's endgame, I returned to my search. I examined a thickly weeded patch next to what we were guessing was Aaron and Quito's picnic spot, and a few minutes later, I was rewarded for my diligence.

Getting to my feet, I held the black rectangular device over my head and shouted, "I think I found Quito's cell phone!"

"That's terrific!" Jake was poking around the tractor but paused to give me a thumbs-up.

Then he did something I couldn't see. A couple of seconds later, he jogged back to where I was standing. In his left hand he held a plastic bag that contained a long wooden stick with a cotton ball on its end.

I pointed to his prize and asked, "What's that?"

"I swabbed the tractor's steering wheel and seat." Jake tucked the baggie away in his jacket pocket. "I'll send it to a friend of mine who works in a private forensic lab and see if she can identify anything unusual."

"You think that the poison that killed Mr. Burgess might have been splashed on him?" I paused at the implications, then frowned and demanded, "Did you touch it?"

"I wore gloves, and yes, I do think the substance that caused his symptoms was probably inhaled."

The cell phone that I'd found was still clutched in my right hand, and as I unfurled my fingers, I said, "What should we do with this?"

"Any idea where Escobar lives?" Jake took the device, and after scrutinizing it, he pressed a few buttons. "Shoot! It's password protected."

I was surprised the phone had enough battery life to work. Quito must be one of those rare people who kept their cells turned off until they needed them.

"Quito mentioned that his place was about halfway between the field that he was working in and the one that our victim was planting." Pointing north, I said, "I'm betting that he lives a few miles that way. There aren't too many houses on this road, and a few days ago, when I delivered a get-well basket out here, the only mobile home that I saw along the way was between the old mill and here."

Jake took my elbow and ushered me toward the pickup. "Let's go take a look."

"Okay." I walked along with him. "But I doubt Quito is there."

"Why do you say that?" Jake waited for me to get settled into the truck, then closed that door and ran around to the driver's side.

Once he was behind the wheel, I explained, "Because that tractor wouldn't be sitting out in the field if Quito wasn't still being held by the sheriff's department."

"Of course." Jake hit his forehead with the palm of his hand. "Even an ancient tractor like that one is too valuable to leave in an isolated field just begging to be stolen or vandalized."

"Right." I nodded. "And it could actually be worth more than you think if it's vintage enough to be a collector's item. Maybe a couple of thousand or more."

"That much?"

I nodded, then got back to figuring out Quito's status with the cops. "Let see, the deputy took Quito over to the sheriff's office yesterday afternoon about five or so, right?" I asked.

Reading my mind, Jake shook his head. "But they won't count him as being in custody until he said he wanted to leave, so we have no idea when they are legally mandated to release him."

In Missouri a person can usually only be held twenty to twenty-four hours without being charged. But the cops have ways around that restriction. I hoped poor Quito had asked for an attorney.

"What should we do with his phone?" I ran a finger over the screen.

"We could bring it to him at the Sheriff's office, but I'd sure like to get a look at its contents before we return it."

I examined the device, but had no better luck than Jake trying to get by the password prompt. I turned it off to save the battery and tucked it into my purse.

"That would be ideal. I really don't think Quito has anything to do with his friend's death, and if we could see his contacts, we might be able to call someone for him. He mentioned that he had a date, so she might have some info."

"We could take the phone to our friendly hacker," Jake suggested. "Did she go back to the club after the meeting with her father?"

"My guess would be yes."

Hmm. Poppy *did* claim she could get into any phone, which I assumed was connected with her almost uncontrollable urge to monitor what was going on around her. She had even strategically placed concealed listening devices all over Gossip Central.

Poppy liked to know what was being said, though she never talked about anything she heard with anyone, except very occasionally Boone and me. It was purely about her need to hold all the power in any situation, which was due to her father's iron-fisted control over her during her childhood.

"Are you okay going to find Poppy before we get something to eat?"

"Sure." My stomach growled, denying my assertion, but I whipped out the granola bar that I'd stashed in my pocket and said, "This will tide me over."

"Let's take a quick run past that trailer you mentioned, then head over to Gossip Central."

When I nodded my agreement with his plan, Jake started the truck and drove it onto the road. A few minutes later, we were at what I assumed was Quito's place. The windows were dark and the driveway was empty.

"I'll go knock just in case." Jake parked and opened his door.

Before he got out, I suggested, "Why don't we slip a letter under his door saying we have his phone. We can put your office phone number for him to contact us."

"Good idea."

Jake waited while I dug through my purse, found a piece of paper and a pen, and wrote down our message. With the note in his hand, he hopped to the ground and marched up the sidewalk.

A few minutes later, he was back in the truck and we were headed toward Gossip Central. Just outside the city limits, its location in that particular area was best for all concerned.

Having a father who was the chief of the Shadow Bend police force could have been tricky for Poppy. However, since her bar wasn't in his jurisdiction, he couldn't be accused of a conflict of interest if there was any criminal activity at the club.

The chief was able to avoid the possibility of his

interfering with the way his daughter ran her business. And Poppy was able to avoid starting another feud with her father.

Jake kept to the speed limit as he drove down the blacktop toward the bar. We passed weathered farmhouses and newly plowed fields, a refreshing change of scenery from the commute to my previous job.

One of the big advantages of changing professions by purchasing the dime store was the peacefulness of the deserted countryside and the lack of traffic and congestion that I'd faced every day when I commuted into Kansas City.

On a Sunday night, the road was nearly deserted. And when we turned into the bar's parking lot, we'd only passed one other vehicle since leaving Quito's mobile home.

A slight breeze caused the sign over the club's entrance to swing on its chains. It swayed gently to and fro, while the open light flashed a welcoming neon green.

I had texted Poppy that we were on our way over, and by the time Jake and I got out of the truck and walked up the steps to the club's entrance, she was waiting at the door. She swung it wide open, beaming our welcome.

With her cobweb of silvery-blond hair, amethyst eyes, and delicate build, many guys believed she was the answer to all their fantasies. They often paid dearly for that mistake and quickly discovered the Poppy was no man's Barbie doll.

Before Jake or I could speak, she put her lips to my ear and whispered, "Boone's here. Just wait until you hear why he was off-grid."

CHAPTER 17
Devereaux

"Boone's in our usual spot," Poppy informed us. "I'll grab us a pitcher of margaritas and meet you guys there." She started to leave, then paused and looked at Jake. "I suppose you want a beer."

"Yes, ma'am." Jake touched the rim of his cowboy hat, "Whatever you have on tap."

"Bring some snacks too!" I called after her as she scurried away. I'd need something in my nearly empty stomach if we would be drinking.

Jake took my elbow and we moved out of the entrance. As we passed the restrooms, I noticed a new sign on the men's room door. OUR AIM IS TO KEEP THIS PLACE CLEAN. YOUR AIM WILL HELP IN THIS MATTER. PLEASE STAND CLOSER TO THE URINALS. YOUR EQUIPMENT IS SHORTER THAN YOU THINK.

Although Jake just shook his head, I was still

giggling when he and I entered the crowded bar area. Gossip Central had started out life as a cattle barn, and instead of making expensive changes, Poppy had used what was already there. The center of the club contained the stage, dance floor, and bar, while the hayloft was now a space that could be rented for private parties.

The stalls had been transformed into secluded settings with comfortable seating and themed decorations. Secluded, that is, except Poppy's concealed listening devices. She swore they were never activated when we were in our preferred little alcove, the one we'd nicknamed the Stable, but I wasn't sure that I believed her.

Boone occupied his customary spot, the saddle-stitched club chair with the matching footstool. He greeted us with a smile. It wasn't as happy and carefree as normal, but his teeth still flashed strikingly white against his tanned face.

He claimed that his skin was naturally that color, however both Poppy and I knew about the sunbed hidden in his back bedroom. We didn't nag him about the health hazards of tanning, and he didn't bring up our indiscretions.

My biggest one was a tiny shooting star tattoo that I had gotten during a college spring break trip to Mexico. Due to its location, as long as I was dressed — even in a bathing suit or just my underwear — it was never visible, but of course by now Jake had seen it. He'd vowed to keep quiet about it. Birdie would kill me, and in order to reassure me, he'd revealed a secret of his own.

Poppy's big secret was how she had gotten the financing for the bar. She'd finally told her father, but he'd begged her not to make the name of her clandestine benefactor public knowledge, so we'd all sworn an oath of silence.

I had a feeling that Boone might have something else he was keeping from us, and while Jake hung up our coats and his hat, I leaned over to give my BFF a reassuring hug.

Before letting go, I asked, "You okay, sweetie?"

He shook his head, knowing he didn't have to pretend with us. "Not really."

"What's going on?" I joined Jake on the brown leather love seat across from where Boone sat, then leaned toward my friend and squeezed his leg.

Before he could answer, Poppy arrived and said, "Boone got here a few minutes before you texted that you guys were coming over." She handed Jake his beer, then placed a tray with three glasses, a pitcher, and a frosty mug on the wood and wrought iron feed box that served as a coffee table. "Boone had already told me a little, but once he knew you two were on your way, he said he'd prefer to wait and only tell his story once."

We all turned to look at Boone, who opened his mouth but closed it when a server rushed around the corner. She had a basket of potato chips, a bowl of nuts, and a platter of salami, cheese, and crackers.

"Thanks, Hayley." Poppy smiled at the young woman who dipped her head in response and then scurried away. Once we were alone, Poppy moved to sit in the chair next to Boone's. Her fanny hadn't even touched the leather seat when she demanded, "Spill!"

"When I got home, I saw your note on my front door." He ran his hands through the swath of tawny-gold hair that fell across his forehead. "So, I know that you figured out that I was on a date. Or at least I was supposed to be on a date."

"You were stood up?" I said gently, patting his leg again.

"Sort of. It's hard to know where to start." Boone poured himself a margarita and took a healthy gulp.

Poppy barely allowed him to swallow before ordering, "Just tell us everything!"

"We'd been seeing each other for a while, and we decided to spend the weekend together." Boone's hazel eyes crinkled. "We've both been super busy, but we swore that we'd take off Saturday afternoon and meet no later than five at this cute boutique hotel in the city that I saw advertised on a legal blog that I read. We planned to stay the night and spend all day Sunday relaxing."

"But she never showed?" Poppy growled. "Tell me who it is and I'll make sure she's sorry she hurt you."

Boone's gaze darted back and forth between Poppy and me, with an occasional peek at Jake before he finally said, "It's not a she and it wasn't his fault."

Jake and I exchanged glances. He had long since suspected that Boone preferred men and had pointed out little things to me that made me wonder if he was right. But when I looked at Poppy, I could tell that she was totally floored.

Which I could definitely understand. We'd known Boone since childhood and he'd always dated women. Usually, very beautiful and accomplished women. If it wasn't for Jake, I would have been just as flabbergasted as Poppy.

"Why haven't you ever told us that before?" Poppy frowned crossing her arms. "You have to know we wouldn't care who you were with as long as that person made you happy."

"That's the thing. I've never believed in happily ever after."

"Which is stupid," Poppy snorted.

I jumped in and pointed out, "We've been over this before. Sure, our immediate families haven't been the best role models. My mom is on husband number five. At least, I think it's five."

"You said that, after you saved your mother from that murder charge, you two kept in touch." Poppy tilted her head. "How can you not know which husband she's on?"

"I still only get a quick text from her once in a while, and she mentions so many men it's hard to figure out if she married them or just lived with them long enough to bleed their bank accounts dry."

"Whatever." Poppy thrust out her chin. "My parents celebrated their thirty-sixth anniversary last June. And my father's been much better about not spending so much time at the police station."

"Good for them. Between my own folks starting to talk to each other and Dev's romance"—Boone stared at Jake, who was holding my hand—"I decided to give love a whirl. But before I told you guys, I had to let Mom and Dad know. And before I did that, I wanted to make sure I really had something special to tell them about."

"So, what happened?" Jake asked.

"I got to the hotel and checked in. Then, I guess because I have been working too hard, I fell asleep." Boone's expression was sheepish. "When I woke up and realized that I was alone, I kept texting Q to see where he was, but he never answered. I was so upset that I drank the entire contents of the minibar and passed out."

Q? A date in the city? Could it be?

Before I could ask, Poppy jumped in and said, "Didn't you see the messages from Dev and me when you woke up? We were really worried when you didn't answer."

"Sorry," Boone apologized. "I didn't come to until a couple of hours ago, and then I just felt so numb that I drove home. A few miles out of Shadow Bend, I finally heard from Q. He'd been held by the cops overnight, and he'd lost his cell so he couldn't call me until he got home, found my business card, then drove to a neighbor's house to use a phone. I told him that if the cops tried to take him in again to tell them that I was his attorney, which I now am, and have them find my number for him."

"You're dating and he didn't know your phone number?" Poppy wrinkled her brow in disbelief.

"Not without his cell." When she continued to frown, he challenged, "Do you have anyone's number memorized anymore, or do you just scroll through your contacts?"

We all nodded our head in acquiescence. The only number I knew by heart was Birdie's, and it had been the same ever since I first learned it.

"Is Q's full name Quito?" I exchanged a glance with Jake, whose stunned expression probably matched mine.

"How did you know that?" Boone stared at me.

"Did you see my first text to you? The one asking if you had any info on Aaron Burgess?" When he shook his head, I continued, "We've been hired to look into his death, which of course is how we met Quito."

Boone frowned. "How did you two get involved in that mess?"

I took a deep breath and explained everything.

Boone was silent as I recapped Saturday's events and what we'd found out about the victim so far, but when I paused for breath, he said, "Q told me about finding Aaron and what happened afterwards, but the part that I don't understand is why the cops think Aaron was murdered."

Jake took over. "Primarily because the docs have ruled out natural causes and the circumstances surrounding his death don't support any accidental application of whatever caused his symptoms. According to Quito, there was nothing at the scene such as insecticide or fertilizer, just the seeds he was planting."

Boone was silent, evidently thinking about what he'd learned, then he demanded, "You don't think Q killed Aaron, do you? Because I can tell you right now, he didn't." Boone glared at me. "He had absolutely no reason to want his friend dead."

"Actually, we believe you," Jake assured him. "But we need to find out what substance killed Burgess, how he was exposed to it, and who gains by his death."

I dug through my purse and produced the cell phone we'd found by the field. "If you happen to know Quito's password, maybe something on here will help us figure out where to look next."

CHAPTER 18
Devereaux

Boone had wanted to drive out to Quito's place and have him unlock the cell phone, but we had persuaded him to wait and let us take a look at the contents first. After texting Noah that he was no longer working for him, Jake presented Boone with an official contract for his services as a private investigator.

Once Boone had signed on the dotted line and handed over a dollar, Jake had promised that anything incriminating that we found on the cell would not be turned over to the police. I wasn't sure if PIs actually had confidentiality privileges or if Jake was stretching the truth in order to reassure Boone. I'd have to look that up sometime.

Pushing legalities aside, I concentrated on our current project, getting around the cell's password protection. Depending on Quito's settings, we only had five to ten attempts to unlock his phone.

Jake asked Boone to start making a list of likely candidates, and while he was lost in thought trying to figure out what combination of letters and numbers Quito would most likely use, the rest of us continued to discuss the case.

"Can't the cops just dust Aaron's tractor for fingerprints?" Poppy asked. "Surely they took Quito's when they had him in custody."

"They wouldn't have to do that. Q was in the army, so they already had access to his prints, not to mention his DNA. You have no idea how much data the government has on all of us." Boone looked up from his notes and wrinkled his nose. "And they never willingly get rid of any of it."

Boone was a wee bit of a conspiracy nut, and I knew I had to stop him before he started in on the fact that Denver International Airport stood above an underground city that served as a headquarters of the New World Order. Or that the true story behind the disappearance of Malaysia Airlines Flight 370 involved the Russians.

As he opened his mouth to propose that the government tracked us through a microchip in our flu vaccinations, I quickly asked him, "How did the sheriff leave things with Quito?"

As the lawyer in our group, Boone would probably have a good idea what the sheriff's actions suggested. Was Quito in real trouble, or were the cops satisfied by his answers to their questions?

"It's hard to say." Boone bit his lip. "A deputy told him not to leave town, then drove him to the Underwood Clinic to get his truck." Boone sighed. "You all know that most of my practice is real estate and divorce, not criminal law. I don't really have an inkling where Q stands with the sheriff."

We all looked at Jake. As an ex-US Marshal, he was our real expert. I should have asked him first.

Jake pursed his lips as he considered his answer, then shrugged. "Depending on what they find out about Burgess and the cause of his death, they could make Quito's life miserable. A lot hinges on how the local sheriff operates and how Quito's background checks out."

"In that regard, as long as they aren't able to access his juvenile records, he should be okay." Boone frowned, then used his thumb to smooth the line between his brows. "And they clearly don't have any evidence against him or they wouldn't have let him go."

"If they did get a look at those juvenile reports, what kind of stuff would they find?" Poppy was never one to back away from the tough questions.

Boone rested his chin on his fist. "Nothing violent. Q grew up poor and got into some of the usual trouble kids with no money and time on their hands don't always manage to avoid. But after he graduated from high school, he enlisted in the army, and he's walked the straight and narrow ever since."

We all sat lost in our thoughts until Poppy said, "I have an idea!" She whipped out her cell and continued, "I used to date one of the deputies. Maybe I can get him to give me a hint of what they have on Quito."

The three of us listened intently as Poppy spoke to her friend. She was persuasive, but the deputy hadn't been involved in the case and didn't have any info to share. He did promise to let her know if he heard anything interesting.

After Poppy hung up, the rest of us sat in frustrated silence while Boone continued to try the passwords from the list that he'd made. Every time he'd enter one that didn't work, his scowl deepened.

My eyes had begun to drift shut when Boone suddenly pumped his fist in the air and said, "Got it. Q's password is 1TURNSUP. It's the name of his first pet, a feral cat he used to feed in the alley behind his mom's apartment."

Boone handed Jake the phone, and while he scrolled through Quito's cell, I poured us all another round of margaritas. Poppy left to get Jake a refill on his beer, and with a lull in the action, I scarfed down half the salami and cheese platter.

Once Poppy returned and helped herself to a handful of nuts, she wiggled her eyebrows and said, "Are you and Marshal McHottie having fun playing house?"

Jake's ears turned as red as the cardinal that frequented Gran's birdfeeder, but he didn't look up from the tiny device in his hand. Poppy knew it embarrassed him when she pointed out that he was attractive, so she made sure that each nickname was more outrageous than the previous one. I was proud of Jake that he took her teasing so well.

I bit back a giggle and winked. "We've hardly had time to enjoy it, but I'm hoping I won't fall asleep quite so early tonight."

"Hey, guys," Boone said. "Could we get serious about this? Q's neck is on the line here."

Poppy rolled her eyes. "You're no fun."

I saw Boone's unhappy expression and stepped in. "What we really need to do is come up with some better suspects than Quito. Ones that the sheriff can't ignore."

"It's always the significant other." Poppy's grin was feline.

Boone immediately leapt to Mrs. Burgess's defense. "Rose wouldn't do something like that." He shook his head. "She's a nice lady who's had some bad luck in life."

"Poppy told me about what happened with that guy she was dating when she was a model." I tapped my fingers on my knee. "Do you have any details about that?"

"No. But Q told me that Aaron told him that she was never the same after that. From what was said, he suspected that there was more to it than this jerk just painting her as the scarlet woman." Boone pursed his lips. "And Aaron should know. They dated in high school, and he kept in touch with her while she was in New York."

"So, she cheated on him with the football player?" Poppy leaned forward, clearly ready for some gossip.

"Not at all." It was obvious that Boone was getting annoyed with Poppy's attitude. "They agreed that a long-distance romance wouldn't work and both were free to see other people."

"Still." Poppy's expression was stubborn. "If Aaron was calling and texting her, he must have had feelings for her and been upset when she was so publicly linked to another man."

"Which would be a motive for him to murder her, but not the other way around." Boone's tone indicated that he was majorly disappointed in Poppy.

"Let's not forget Mrs. Burgess flew out of town that morning," I reminded them.

"We need to find out what time her flight left." Poppy crossed her arms. "And what time Aaron was poisoned, to see if she had a window of opportunity."

"That last one will be tough." Jake looked up from Quito's phone. "If Burgess was dosed with something, it could be anywhere from after he and Quito ate lunch to when Quito returned looking for his phone."

"Which puts it between twelve thirty and three." I tapped my chin. "If Mrs. Burgess left for the airport in the morning, I doubt she'd be anywhere close enough to spray her husband with a toxic substance in the early afternoon."

"I'm keeping her on the list until we find out for sure when she was in KC and when Aaron was killed." Poppy dramatically produced a pen from her jean pocket and picked up a paper napkin.

It made me wonder what my friend had against Rose. Could it be that the woman had been a successful model in New York? It wasn't often Poppy ran into anyone who might be a rival in terms of looks. Maybe she was jealous.

"How about someone who wanted Aaron's land?" Jake suggested.

"That would mean Q's in danger too!" Boone's eyes widened and he clutched his chest.

"Boone, take a breath," I admonished. "Jake's just brainstorming."

"And since he's a partner and Rose will inherit, if someone wanted that land, they have to be prepared to kill three people for it," Poppy added.

I shifted in my seat. "Unless the murderer believed Rose and Quito would be more willing to sell if Aaron was gone."

"Then put that sleazy Harris Josephson on your list," Boone ordered. "Although Q's never mentioned any offers, Josephson has been trying to buy up a lot of the smaller farms to sell as a package to one of those mega-farm companies. I've had a lot of clients calling me and complaining that he's been harassing them to sell."

Poppy inked the words *Harris Josephson* on her list, then said, "I almost forgot. About six weeks ago, Aaron was in Gossip Central, and he and Josh Camilo got into a scuffle. I don't know how it ended because I made them take it outside."

"What was the fight about?" Jake asked.

"It might have been something about one of them owing the other money." Poppy shrugged. "Raised voices aren't exactly out of the ordinary around here, so I didn't pay that much attention."

"Can you remember who else was around when Burgess and Camilo were arguing?" Jake asked.

When Poppy shook her head, I slid a glance at Jake. He didn't approve of my BFF's surveillance system. If we couldn't find out any other way, I'd ask her if she might have a recording of Aaron's tussle with Josh. But I'd do it when Jake wasn't around.

"You know," Poppy said, tapping a fingernail against her lips, "we're making this all about Aaron, but maybe someone wanted Rose for himself."

"That football guy, Brandon Tate," Boone said. "But didn't he fade from the picture once all that mess was spread across the tabloids?"

"Until recently," Poppy informed us, nearly wiggling with glee. "Evidently, Jerkface's wife finally got fed up and divorced him. He was on some reality show not too long ago crying about how Rose had been the love of his life."

CHAPTER 19
Devereaux

Jake looked up from Quito's phone and said, "At first glance, I don't see anything on here that gives me any kind of a lead to follow regarding Burgess's death." He turned to Boone. "I'd like to read off his list of contacts, and you can tell me what you know about them."

Poppy and I looked at each other uncomfortably. I wasn't sure that I'd want to hear who was on the contact list of a newish love interest, and from the expression on Poppy's face, she was in the don't ask, don't tell camp too.

Boone chuckled at our reaction, then reached over and patted both our knees. "I'm not worried that Q was seeing someone behind my back."

"We weren't worried about that." I fought to keep the sheepishness I felt from showing in my voice.

"Liar." Poppy leaned forward and punched me lightly in the arm. "That was exactly what we were worried about."

"Fine." I blew away a curl that had drifted into my eyes.

Jake cleared his throat and started reading names off Quito's cell phone. Boone was able to identify them all and most were pretty standard. Parents, siblings, cousins, doctors, dentists, and businesses associated with the farm.

But when Jake said, "Blake Laudon," Boone turned up his nose and said, "Really? I'm surprised he's on the list."

"Why? What's wrong with him?" Poppy drummed her long red nails on her black-denim-clad knee.

Boone sniffed, "He's an old army buddy of both Q and Aaron."

"And that's a bad thing?" I was still hungry, so I started in on the potato chips.

"Not usually." Boone sneered. "But apparently he felt slighted when Aaron invited Q to invest in the farm instead of him."

"Interesting," Jake murmured. "What happened?"

"The three of them had been tight, but Q had more agricultural experience, so Aaron approached him first," Boone explained. "When Blake found out, he got all pissy about it and stopped talking to them both."

Jake showed Boone the phone. "It looks as if he called Quito sometime last week."

"He probably butt-dialed," Boone scoffed. "From what Q told me, Aaron hadn't even considered asking Blake because he was such a city boy. Then when Aaron tried to apologize, Blake accused him of all kinds of awful things."

"Hmm." Poppy sucked the end of her pen. "Was he as mad at Quito?"

"His was more guilt by association, so I guess not." Boone bit his lip and looked at Jake. "We'll have to ask Q about this, won't we?"

"We should." Jake nodded. "I can just approach this Laudon guy without talking to Quito first, but that's not the best tactic."

"Well." Boone got up and swiped at an imaginary speck of dust on a bridle hanging on the plank wall. Without looking over at us, he asked, "Can you leave out the part where I figured out Q's password?"

"I could."

I recognized the look in Jake's eye and braced myself for the bomb he was about to drop. "But since you hired me on his behalf, that's probably ethically shady on both our parts."

"I think we crossed that line when I got you into his phone." Boone turned his head and stared at Jake.

Time to step in. "Boone, sweetie, you need to be honest with Quito. Jake and I will do the best we can to make sure the sheriff arrests the right person, but it will be a lot tougher if you make us tiptoe around the truth."

"There's only one flaw in that plan." Boone's shoulders sagged. "What if I lose Q because of it?"

"He's right." Poppy poked me in the shoulder. "People don't always appreciate you doing what's best for them."

"True." I scowled at her. She wasn't helping. "But better Boone tells Q himself than he finds out some other way."

"Fine." Boone squirmed. "But I want to see him alone first."

"All right." Jake nodded. "I need to get Devereaux some real nourishment before she goes into a snack-food coma." He grinned at me as I hastily dropped the handful of chips that had been on the way to my mouth back into the bowl.

"Then Q and I will meet you at your office tomorrow at noon." Boone cleared his throat. I could almost see the lump that was stuck there as he muttered, "That is, if Q is still speaking to me."

Poppy's expression was sympathetic as she murmured, "It'll be okay."

Before Boone could respond to her assurance, his cell rang. He snatched it from his pocket and swiped it on. As he listened, he jumped up and grabbed his coat.

Hanging up, Boone said, "I've got to go. That was Quito. He borrowed one of the firefighter's phones to call me. His trailer is burning down."

CHAPTER 20
Devereaux

With Boone in the lead behind the wheel of his parents' Volvo, Poppy's ginormous silver Hummer hugging his bumper, and Jake's truck bringing up the rear, we looked like some kind of odd parade going down the narrow asphalt road toward Quito's place. I knew Jake had only had a beer and a half, and Poppy rarely drank more than a couple of cocktails, but I was worried about Boone's driving ability.

Although there was a possibility that he'd only had the two margaritas that I saw him consume, but that was a big question mark. In his emotional state, even that much alcohol could impair his reaction time. With everything else going on, we sure didn't need him to be pulled over by the cops. Not to mention, the frightening thought of him crashing the car and getting hurt.

Jake, Poppy, and I had all tried to persuade him to ride with one of us, but he refused and hopped in the Volvo before we could grab him or the keys. Our only recourse was to follow him and pray for the best.

While Boone had assured us that he could handle picking up Quito on his own, Poppy and I wouldn't dream of letting our friend do this by himself. Jake probably had another reason for accompanying Boone to the scene, but I didn't ask about his motives and he didn't volunteer.

I never thought that I'd hear Poppy say it, but she'd actually admitted that she wished Quito's place was located in her father's jurisdiction. We agreed with her on that point. Having the sheriff's department involved while Quito was their prime suspect for Aaron Burgess's murder was a hot mess waiting to happen.

Due to the rural area where the trailer was parked—not in the city limits but a long way from the county seat—the Shadow Bend Fire Company was the department tasked with responding. This was a stroke of luck for our little group, because the fire chief, Cooper McCall, was dating our friend Veronica Ksiazak.

When he'd first come to town, his rugged good looks had attracted the local female population like bread crumbs to a duck. His popularity with the ladies had made me wary, but once I got to know Coop, I realized that he and my friend Ronni would be a good match, and I'd set them up on a date.

They'd hit it off and immediately become exclusive. Jake and I had doubled with Ronni and

Coop on several occasions. He had a lot of southern charm, and Ronni had a sharp wit that kept us all in stitches. Plus, it was just nice to socialize with another couple.

As we approached Quito's small driveway and I saw it and his tiny front lawn was full of emergency equipment, I hoped our friendship with Coop would result in his cooperation regarding any pertinent information about the fire. Or if not exactly cooperation, at least a little willingness to share.

Because Quito's property was so crowded, we were left with the side of the road as our sole parking option. Boone pulled in first, with Poppy right behind him. Jake made a perfect three-point turn and stopped the truck on the opposite shoulder from my friends.

Happy as I was that we had arrived safely, I dreaded what we would find. The mobile home we had visited earlier in the afternoon was now little more than a charred metal rectangle.

My stomach churned as I opened the pickup's door. What on earth had happened? Was this a horrible accident or was it connected to the murder?

I don't believe in coincidences, and we'd just heard that there was someone who had a grudge against both Quito and Aaron. All Boone had told us while running to his parents' car was that Quito had been in his truck headed to the Burgess residence to talk to Rose when he heard a whooshing sound. He'd looked in his rearview mirror, seen flames leaping into the sky, and had immediately driven back to his place. By the time he'd arrived, his home was engulfed in a raging fire.

Coop must have seen our little procession, because he met the four of us near the road and asked, "What are y'all doing out here?" His tanned forehead creased in puzzlement.

Although Coop had lived in a lot of different places when he was in the marines, he was originally from Georgia and still had the accent to prove it. Even in his oversized gear, Copper McCall was an extremely attractive man. Tall, with well-developed muscles and a great smile, he was a lot of women's fantasy firefighter.

"Where's Quito?" Boone demanded.

Coop's expression didn't change, but I did notice a flicker of understanding in his brown eyes, then he pointed to an ambulance and said, "He's getting checked out. He ran into the fire to save his dog."

My heart thudded at the possibility of an injured animal, and I asked, "Did he? Save it, I mean?"

"Yep." He gestured toward the ambulance again. "They're both being given oxygen, but they seem okay."

Boone pushed past us and headed toward Quito and his pet.

With him gone, a lot of the emotion drained from the situation, and Jake stepped forward. "Any idea how the fire started?"

"My first guess would be a spark from a frayed

cord. Other possibilities are an aftermarket charging cable or a power strip without surge protection or a damaged outlet." Coop frowned. "Or a device that overheated while charging. Most people don't realize how hot those items get or that they should be placed on cool, hard surfaces while plugged in."

"Would an electrical fire cause a whooshing sound?" Poppy asked.

"No, that would more likely be from a natural gas leak or if fuel was used as an accelerant." Coop took off his gloves and stuffed them into his pocket. "No one said anything about hearing a whooshing sound."

Poppy jerked her head toward the two men embracing near the ambulance. "Quito told Boone on the phone that he heard one."

Poppy opened her mouth to go on, but Jake cut her off by asking, "When will you be able to determine if this is arson versus an accident?"

"A simple fire can be handled pretty quickly, but a major one can sometimes take months." Coop transferred his helmet from his left hand to his right, then wiped the sweat off his forehead with the back of his arm. "It really depends on how much evidence and witness information the investigator has to sort through to determine the cause."

I glanced at Jake, questioning whether we should inform Coop about the murder. He shrugged, obviously on the fence about sharing the information.

Realizing that Coop would hear about it sooner

or later and figuring it was best to keep on his good side so he'd continue to cooperate with us, I said, "One thing that might be important in the investigation is that Quito's business partner, Aaron Burgess, died on Saturday from some mysterious poison that has yet to be identified."

"You pulling my chain?" Coop's eyebrows rose. "That sounds more like a television show than something that would happen in a small town."

I hurriedly summarized the events, then added, "We have no idea of how the pieces fit together, but Boone has hired Jake's PI services to look into Aaron's death, and I'm guessing he'll be adding Quito's fire to the contract."

"Wow!" Coop turned his back and started toward Boone and Quito.

Poppy trotted after him. I followed her, and Jake wasn't far behind me.

Coop double-timed across the lawn until he arrived at the ambulance, where he looked at the EMT and asked, "Is Mr. Escobar okay to answer some questions?"

"As far as I can tell." The woman shrugged. "He's declined to be transported to the hospital, and he signed off on his decision, so he's all yours."

Coop turned to Quito, took a small notebook from his inside breast pocket, and flipped it open, then said, "Tell me how you first became aware of the fire and what you did after that."

"I was on my way to pay a condolence call,"

Quito started, then stuttered to a stop and glanced at Boone, who nodded for him to continue.

While Quito told Coop about Aaron's death and his experiences on Saturday, I tuned out and thought about what we knew so far. It wasn't much.

We really needed to interview the suspects that we'd come up with during our brainstorming session. But before that, we had to determine the exact cause of Aaron's death, especially the name of the poison and how it was administered.

When Coop finished with his questions and walked away, I focused back to the present. Boone had his arm around Quito and was leading him and his dog toward where we had all parked.

Poppy, Jake, and I followed them, and as Quito and his dog got into Boone's car, Jake asked, "When did Mrs. Burgess arrive home?"

"I'm not sure." Quito blinked, the shock of the past couple of days apparent in his expression. "I called her right after the first time I called Boone. She told me that she was home and that I should come over when I could."

Glancing at Jake, I raised my brows. How had she gotten back so fast?

<u>CHAPTER 21</u>
Devereaux

I had spent Monday morning cleaning my new home and doing laundry. Jake and Tony had done a fair job keeping the place tidy, but the kitchen and bathrooms had been in desperate need of a good deep scrubbing, and I wasn't sure that either man understood the necessity of moving objects off the surfaces they dusted.

After a quick lunch, Jake and I headed into town, arriving at the dime store a few minutes before twelve. I'd immediately started working on gift basket orders, and he'd headed upstairs to the office suite he rented from my company to use for his private detective business.

In addition to the space Jake occupied, the second floor held a teen lounge where the afterschool crowd could chill out. Provided, of course, they bought their drinks and munchies from my soda fountain.

It was a win-win situation. Instead of hanging around the dime store and getting in the way of me or my customers, they had a previously underutilized area all to themselves where they could talk, flirt, and play games.

Right now, both the store and the teen lounge were empty. But come three o'clock, that would change dramatically. And about ten minutes before that happened, my student clerk, Taryn Wenzel, would show up.

On the recommendation of Mrs. Zeigler, the high school principal, I had hired Taryn from the vocational education program. After losing my two previous clerks—one to college and one for less auspicious reasons—I'd had to take on a couple of new staff members.

My father was filling the full-time vacancy and Taryn the part-time position. They both were good with the adolescent crowd, and I left the supervision of the teen lounge to whichever of them was working with me that day.

Boone had called and said he and Quito would be over to discuss the case around one. While we waited for them, Jake was doubtlessly upstairs busy making calls regarding Aaron Burgess's murder.

I, on the other hand, was lost in thoughts of sensual darkness and guilty pleasures as I contemplated the basket that I had been making for the last hour. It was one of my erotic specialties, so I kept glancing at the door, prepared to throw a sheet over it if one of my more prudish customers came into the store.

Examining the bachelorette basket, I knew something was missing. It needed that extra zing to be amazing. The bridesmaids had asked that I turn up the heat, and so far, I had included pheromone body lotion, edible finger paints, and a deck of playing cards with fifty-two different sexual positions.

All the goodies were nestled in the folds of a red satin robe for the bride and a pair of matching sleep pants for the groom. I was considering a box of chocolate-dipped strawberries, but that seemed so cliché. What was the final item that would wow them?

I leaned a hip against the old kitchen table I used as a workbench and let my mind wander. Of course, I would place my signature item—the perfect book for the recipient—in a prominent position. The tome that I had selected for this one was *The Erotic Edge: 22 Erotic Stories for Couples* by Lonnie Barbach. But what else did this basket need?

Pursing my lips, I thought about the bridal couple. He was a veterinarian and she was the CEO of a successful tech company. Both were in their late thirties.

Ah ha! This basket required a sophisticated touch to finish it off. And I had just the item. It was costly, but the bridesmaids had told me not to skimp.

I knelt down and began searching my bins for the velvet box holding the Crave Droplet Necklace that I had purchased a few months ago. It was a long stainless-steel chain ending in two pendants, each of which was equipped with a small motor that was operated with a twist. The adult toy could be worn publicly without anyone having a clue as to its function.

My hunt was interrupted by the jingling of sleigh bells. I swiftly stood, covered my worktable, and hurried to the front counter to greet my first customer of the day.

Sadly, I was willing to bet that the stern-faced middle-aged man who had just entered the store was not a shopper. His cold gray eyes skimmed me from head to foot, and his cheeks hollowed out in disapproval.

The fact that he was wearing a uniform also gave me a hint that he wasn't here to buy a crochet hook or stock up on Ball canning jars.

I met his gaze with a cool look of my own, then in my most professional tone asked, "May I help you?"

He marched between the two paperback bookracks, passed the three-stool soda fountain and the glass candy case, heading straight toward me. It was a little unnerving that he hadn't even glanced at the enticing display of spring candy. What kind of person didn't notice pastel-flowered pretzel bites or rainbow-sprinkled caramel apples?

With his barrel chest and rigid movements, he resembled Brian Dennehy in *First Blood*. I had never seen the county sheriff, but I had a feeling this was the guy. He seemed a little too old and a little too intimidating to be just one of the deputies.

As I considered pushing the button under the register that would summon Jake, the guy continued to advance until the only thing between us was the counter.

Tilting his head, he inquired, "Devereaux Sinclair?"

"Yes." Why was the sheriff asking for me? To cover my consternation, I put on my best don't-mess-with-me expression, the one I'd learned working in the cutthroat investment consulting business, then said, "And you are?"

"Sheriff Kruse."

"Nice to meet you." I had been correct as to his identity.

Impassively, he stated, "I understand you stopped by the sheriff department on Saturday."

"That's correct," I answered slowly, my heart racing. This couldn't be good. "My fiancé and I were trying to locate Quito Escobar to return his possessions."

"How well do you know Mr. Escobar?"

"Not very. I'd met him for the first time that day." I didn't add that since that time I had learned he was dating my BFF. "Why do you ask?"

The sheriff ignored my question. "But you were aware that Mr. Escobar had been present when his friend became ill?"

"Yes." I felt my stomach clench. "My fiancé and I were at Dr. Underwood's clinic, which is how we ended up with Mr. Escobar's possessions. He forgot them when he accompanied his friend to the hospital."

"But if you didn't know Mr. Escobar, why would you go to the trouble to drive all the way over to the county seat just to return his property?" Sheriff Kruse's voice had developed an insinuating purr.

What had I told the deputy? Something about being in the area to eat.

"We were headed that way anyway." I crossed my fingers that my story would match up. "We had reservations at a restaurant there."

"Right." He consulted a small notepad. "But I believe since that time, your acquaintance with Mr. Escobar has become more personal."

"Not really." I tugged at the collar of my peach sweatshirt, suddenly wishing I had on one of the power suits I used to wear daily at my previous job.

"But you showed up at Mr. Escobar's trailer after it went up in flames."

This was beginning to feel like déjà vu. I'd had a cop interrogate me in my store a few years ago. He'd been determined to pin a murder on me. Although I was pretty sure the sheriff wasn't after me, it still felt as if I was walking through a minefield blindfolded.

Clasping my hands together to stop them from shaking, I carefully answered, "I was with Mr. Escobar's attorney when he called to tell him about the fire."

"Which doesn't explain why you'd go out to the

site." Kruse's tone was light, but his expression reminded me of Banshee right before the Siamese cat pounced on an unsuspecting mouse. The sheriff prodded, "Surely, you have better things to do with your time."

I glanced longingly at the rear staircase, wishing Jake would magically appear. But I hadn't gotten an MBA from a top university or survived working in the investment field to resort to summoning a man to rescue me.

So far, Kruse had been civil, so I kept my voice mild. "That may be true, but I don't really understand why my actions are of interest to the county sheriff's department."

"As you're well aware"—Kruse's smile looked as if he was getting a headache—"Mr. Burgess's death was under suspicious circumstances, which we are now investigating."

"Yes." My nails bit into my flesh as I tightened my entwined fingers. "But I still don't see where I come into it."

Minutes went by as we stared at each other, and when I didn't break the growing silence, Kruse blew out a frustrated breath. "We believe that there is a good chance that Mr. Escobar is somehow involved."

"Okay." I was prepared for something like that, but I had wanted the sheriff to admit it.

As my mind flipped through the questions I should ask, Kruse hit me with what he obviously thought was a bombshell. "Are you aware that Mr.

Escobar is a homosexual?"

"I am." *Damn!* If the sheriff was bringing up Quito's love life, did he know Quito was dating Boone? "Why is that anyone's business?"

Kruse nostrils flared. "Because it gives Mr. Escobar a motive to kill Aaron Burgess."

"Really?" I kept my expression neutral, but I was becoming more worried by the second that, somehow, Boone would be caught in this mess. "Were they a couple? I believe Mr. Burgess had a wife."

"Are you telling me you've never heard of a married man having an affair?" Kruse's pupils dilated.

"True, but wouldn't that mean Mrs. Burgess would be more of a suspect than Mr. Escobar?"

"Are you mocking me, Ms. Sinclair?" Kruse's tone was even, but his face was getting red.

Trying to keep on his good side, I said, "Not at all. But wouldn't the wife have more motive than the lover?"

"Possibly," he conceded, then squared his shoulders. "But she has an alibi and Escobar does not."

"Mrs. Burgess was already on her flight out?" He seemed to be in a sharing mood, so I decided to get what info I could out of him.

"No. But she was in Kansas City. She'd checked into work before her husband became ill." Kruse held up his hand before I could speak, then continued, "And there's no way she could have made the round trip back to Shadow Bend and still been on time for her flight."

"Just because she's eliminated doesn't mean Mr. Escobar is guilty."

I didn't like how my voice squeaked, or the fact that my knees had started shaking, but there wasn't anything I could do about either one. When I thought of how upset Boone would be, it was hard to control my own emotions.

"It doesn't." Kruse's tone was hard. "But right now, he is our best suspect."

"But how—" I cleared my throat. "Have you identified the poison and figured out how it was administered?"

"I'm afraid I can't share that information." Kruse twitched his shoulders as if angry at himself for what he'd already revealed. Finally, he continued, "Now why were you really at that fire?"

I stared at him without responding. Should I admit Jake's company was working for Quito? Or...

"Dr. Underwood asked my fiancé to look into Mr. Burgess's poisoning."

Kruse's light gray predatory eyes studied me for a long moment. "Why would he do that?"

Beads of sweat formed on my upper lip as I struggled with what to divulge.

"Ms. Sinclair?" Kruse tapped the countertop as if to get my attention. "It's a simple question."

I lifted my chin and answered, "Dr. Underwood was concerned that the poison might be a danger to the community, and my fiancé is an ex-US Marshal who now operates a private investigation business."

What I failed to mention was that I worked with Jake and that Noah was no longer our client. No way was I disclosing that Boone had hired us on behalf of Quito.

"How public minded." Kruse barely hid his sneer.

"If you check around, you'll find that Dr. Underwood has an extremely philanthropic reputation."

"We will certainly do that." Kruse plucked a chocolate from the basket near the register and unwrapped it. "So, you and your fiancé went out to the fire because he'd been hired by Dr. Underwood."

"Hmm." I was trying to be noncommittal so as to avoid lying to the sheriff.

Kruse popped the candy into his mouth. "I suppose that means I need to talk to your fiancé."

"There's not much he can tell you." I noticed the sheriff didn't offer to pay for the truffle.

"But since I'm here…" Kruse glanced upward. "And Jake Del Vecchio's office is right upstairs…"

The sheriff was sharper than I'd thought. He'd known about Jake all along, and now I wondered if he knew that we were no longer employed by Noah.

I leaned a hip nonchalantly against the counter. "Feel free to go on up."

Kruse's smile sent a chill up my back, and I was

about to hit the panic button when he said, "I think I'll just do that. Why don't you join me?"

"I have to keep an eye on the store."

"It doesn't look too busy." Kruse made a show of peering down each of the empty aisles.

"Fine." Normally, I wouldn't have been so accommodating, but he'd aroused my curiosity, and anyway, as he pointed out, it wasn't as if I would be losing business by closing up for a little while. "I'll just turn over the open sign and lock the door." When he didn't move, I waved at the staircase. "See you in a few minutes."

As soon as he headed toward the rear of the store, I grabbed my cell and typed a hasty text to Jake warning him about the sheriff's imminent arrival.

I then composed a lengthier version, including what Kruse had asked me and what I had answered. Once that was sent, I dialed Boone.

I needed to warn him what was going on. I also needed to stop him and Quito from arriving before the sheriff left. My heart pounded while the phone rang and rang.

CHAPTER 22
Devereaux

Boone going radio silent was becoming a bad habit. He hadn't answered his cell, landline, or business phone, and I'd had to leave a message. Worried that he might not receive it in time, I had to come up with another way to stop him from using his keys to get into the store.

Finally, I'd resorted to taping a cryptic note on the front door that said: THIS IS NOT A DRILL.

Poppy had invented that code when the three of us were in school together. It meant danger ahead and warned the recipient not to continue whatever they were doing. It had mostly been used when teachers were approaching or there was a bully around the corner.

I couldn't remember any of us using it in the past ten years or so. But advertising to my customers that the sheriff was paying the dime store a visit wasn't exactly good for my business.

Which meant in today's situation, signaling with our code seemed like a smart solution to the problem. After all, I needed to warn Boone before he stumbled into a situation best avoided.

Having done all that I could to stop him, I headed to the stairs. As I climbed the steps, I heard the low buzz of voices in conversation.

A few seconds later, when I approached the open door of Jake's office, I saw the sheriff standing near the deer antler hat rack to the right of the entrance. He was inspecting it closely while making admiring sounds.

Jake's cowboy hat hung from the tip of one of the horns that had been mounted on barn wood, and Kruse gestured to it, "The El President is what I wear too. I tried the Shasta, but there was no comparison."

"My uncle Tony bought me my first Stetson, a Tahoe, when I was twelve." Jake sat behind his rustic walnut desk in a massive leather chair. "And he got me this one when I joined the marshals."

"My father gave me my first one when I was about that age too." The sheriff walked over to a pair of antler and cowhide Western chairs and sat down. "I wanted to go to work for the FBI, but the county sheriff has been a Kruse since 1821, and I'm an only child so…"

"Yep." Jake's tone was sympathetic. "Family always comes first."

Kruse nodded, then gestured to the taupe walls that held sepia-tinted photographs of the Old West.

"I'd like to get some of those for my office. Do you mind telling me where you found them?"

While the men bonded over artwork and chatted about estate sales, I entered the office and took the remaining seat. As they continued to talk, I admired my fiancé's arresting good looks and ogled the way his broad chest filled out his shirt.

All too soon, Jake and Kruse finished their decorating discussion, and Jake gave me a slight nod. I interpreted that gesture as meaning he'd seen my text.

More for the sheriff's benefit than Jake's, I announced, "Sheriff Kruse invited me to join him while he talked to you about Aaron Burgess's death."

Jake raised his brows and waited for the sheriff to begin. Although I was brimming with questions, I followed Jake's example and kept quiet.

Kruse went over the same ground with Jake that he'd already covered with me, then asked, "If I were to assure Dr. Underwood that there is no threat to the community, do you feel that he would agree to have you terminate your investigation?"

While Jake formulated his answer, I studied the strong column of his throat as it rose from the collar of his blue-and-green-plaid Western-style shirt. He twitched his broad shoulders, straining the flannel fabric, then he smoothed his palms down his faded jeans, emphasizing his drool-worthy thighs. I barely stopped myself from salivating.

"How would you convince Underwood that the

town was safe?" Jake's voice snapped me out of my lust-filled reverie.

"You don't think he'd take my word for it?" The sheriff frowned.

"Doctors like proof." Jake's tone conveyed the fact that he wasn't a fan of Noah's.

Kruse blew out an exasperated sigh. "I'd need your unqualified assurance that you, Ms. Sinclair, and the doctor will not share this information."

Jake nodded and I raised my hand and said, "Absolutely. It won't leave this room."

Kruse paused dramatically then said, "The forensic lab has pinpointed the poison that Burgess inhaled."

I caught Jake's slight smile. Knowing the identity of the toxin, Jake wouldn't have to mail the sample he'd gotten from the tractor to his friend's lab. That would save Quito a few bucks.

"What was it?" I asked.

Kruse glanced at me, then turned to Jake. "It's malathion."

"I've heard of that." Jake had begun taking notes. "Isn't it a pesticide?"

"It is," Kruse answered. "It's often sprayed on plants to protect them from harmful insects. You can get it in any hardware store, tractor supply, or gardening center."

"Are you saying Burgess was caught during a crop-dusting?" Jake asked, a furrow forming between his dark brows. "Aren't people warned to stay out of the field when that's about to take place?"

Kruse straightened the crease on his uniform pants. "They are. In fact, the EPA requires that at least twelve hours pass between the time of application and commencing of any work in the field."

"Mr. Escobar mentioned that Mr. Burgess was pushing hard because of the wet spring, so he might have ignored the warning," I murmured, then shook my head. "But they were just starting to plant. There weren't any crops to spray."

"Exactly." Kruse leaned forward. "And there weren't any scheduled crop-dusting flights for anywhere nearby."

Jake crossed his arms. "Someone deliberately sprayed him."

"That is my working theory." Kruse pursed his mouth. "Which means he was murdered."

"You've been assuming that all along, haven't you?" I raised a brow.

"Pretty much," Kruse admitted. "Although, there was a brief glimmer of hope when the lab identified the toxic substance. But then, like you pointed out, I realized there was no way Burgess's exposure could have been an accident."

"I see." Tapping my fingernails on the arm of the chair, I considered what that might mean for Quito.

While I was thinking, Kruse stared at Jake and said, "You have to admit that this is not a community threat. There is no reason for Dr. Underwood to continue your employment."

"Maybe not," Jake murmured. "However, what if Burgess was not a targeted victim and this is someone who intends to strike again?"

Kruse jerked as if he'd been slapped. "Don't even say that in jest."

"Serial killers are rare but not unheard of." Jake waited a beat, then he rose from his seat and walked to the door. Kruse followed suit. "Let me talk to Dr. Underwood and I'll get back to you."

"I'll expect to hear from you by end of business today." The sheriff handed Jake his card. "My cell number is on the back." He nodded at me, shot Jake one last glance, then left.

Once Kruse was gone, I said, "Were you just yanking his chain about the serial killer angle?"

"A tad." Jake moved in front of me, took my hands, and pulled me to my feet. "I do want a good excuse to keep investigating, so the sheriff doesn't realize we're working for Escobar."

"But?" I kept pace with Jake as he headed downstairs.

"But there always is that slim possibility that there's some sick douchebag out there getting his jollies by spraying people with a toxic pesticide."

CHAPTER 23
Devereaux

Gone? I mouthed the word to Jake and widened my eyes. Who would have thought that was even a possibility?

Following a brief trip downstairs, I was back in Jake's office. A few seconds after the sheriff left, Boone had sent me a message asking me if it was safe for them to come in. He explained that they were parked out front, keeping an eye on the front entrance, and had seen Kruse drive off.

Once I'd unlocked the door for Boone and Quito, I realized that I couldn't keep the store closed any longer. However, since I was unwilling to miss the next discussion, I'd called my father and asked him to come in a couple of hours earlier than his usual shift.

Luckily, he'd been at A Pretty Picture, his girlfriend Catherine's art gallery, which, like my store, was also on the town square, and he came right over. If he'd been out at the farm, it would have taken him longer to arrive, and I might have missed the interesting fact that Quito had just divulged.

"Don't you think that Rose Burgess flying away this morning is an important piece of information that you might have shared with me?" Boone snapped at his boyfriend.

Evidently, all was not peachy keen between the dating couple.

Quito frowned. "Not really. Rose told me last night before the fire, and with everything happening, I didn't give it a second thought."

"Can you recap that conversation with Mrs. Burgess?" Jake glanced up from his notes.

"Well, I called her from my neighbor's house, and she said she was home. She suggested that I come by right then and pick up the key, because she had to fly out the next morning and wanted me to feed their dog." Quito thrust out his chin. "She couldn't get anyone to cover for her on her job, so she had to fly back to Rome to work the flight returning to New York that she had been scheduled to handle."

I wrinkled my forehead as I tried to unravel Quito's explanation. Evidently, Rose had flown to Rome Saturday morning working her regular shift. Then, either that evening or the next morning, she'd received notice that her husband was dead and hopped on a flight to Kansas City. And now she'd flown back to Rome to work the return leg of her shift.

At least, I think that's what Quito was saying. But if that was true, the hours Rose would have spent in the air made my head spin. And were there even flights from KC to Rome, or did she have to spend even more time changing planes?

"Which airline is she employed by?" Jake asked.

"Uh." Quito wrinkled his brow. "I'm not sure. Let me think."

"Seriously?" The disbelieving word escaped before I could stop myself.

This was Boone's boyfriend, and I didn't want to screw things up for him. But *geez, Louise!* How could the guy not know who his business partner's wife worked for?"

Noticing that my fingers were drumming an agitated rhythm on my thigh, I stilled them. The espresso that I had downed between the sheriff's departure and joining the guys upstairs must have just kicked in.

"Rose works for a private carrier." Quito licked his lips.

Well, that explained how she got back home as fast as she had. The company probably made arrangements to fly her directly here.

"Which airline?" Jake asked, pen poised to make a note of the name.

"I can't remember exactly what it's called. Joystick or Glass Cockpit or…" He scratched his chin. "I know the name was something suggestive."

"Why suggestive?" Jake's impassive voice cut me off before I could make a comment that I'd regret.

"Here's the thing." Quito sighed. "When Rose left modeling, she had quite a bit of money socked away in investments, but she'd been poor most of her life and was afraid to touch her savings. However, she didn't have a lot of education or experience that would get her a decently paying job."

"Okay." Jake stretched out the word, indicating that Quito should continue.

Recalling what Poppy had told me, I thought maybe Quito was at a loss for how to explain the situation.

So, I chimed in, "She didn't go to college or have any marketable skills other than her beauty. And most careers that rely heavily on good looks can be a bit questionable. Is that what you're saying?"

"Right." Quito nodded. "But one of Rose's model friends was married to a pilot who worked for a private carrier, and it turns out that the flight attendants for those airlines don't have to have experience as a commercial flight attendant. It's more about being able to give wealthy clients the high-end service they expect."

"And being charming," I suggested.

"Rose had been living the rich and famous life," Jake said slowly. "Plus, she probably had the connections to secure the luxuries that people who fly private airlines expect."

"Exactly." Quito beamed at us as if Jake were his star pupil. "I remember one guy demanded an artist who would paint his family's portrait during the flight. And another wanted a tiger cub for his children to play with as they jetted to their vineyard in France."

"Wow!" I blinked.

Quito nodded at my amazement. "Those types of expectations are also the reason that, even if her husband had just died, Rose couldn't just blow off work."

"Why is that?" I asked.

"Her job is never secure. A zillion other women want to fly around with rich clients and visit exotic places." Quito shrugged. "Not to mention the huge tips."

"Does the sheriff know she left the country?" Jake asked, drumming his pen on the yellow legal pad he'd been using to take notes.

"Yeah." Quito nodded. "According to Rose, the sheriff wasn't too concerned with her whereabouts because she had an alibi that covered the time of Aaron's death."

"Hmm." Jake continued tapping his Bic. "On to the three possible suspects on our list."

"Suspects?" Quito brightened. "That has to help my case, right?"

Boone patted his boyfriend's hand. "It should. Unless they have alibis too."

"Which would be easier to confirm if the sheriff knew how and when the toxic substance was sprayed on Burgess," I muttered.

Jake had shared what the sheriff had told us as

soon as Quito and Boone arrived. Quito had confirmed our guess that there was no legitimate reason that there would be crop-dusting anywhere near his and Aaron's land.

Now Quito said, "It just dawned on me that, if it had been a crop duster, we should check to see if the entire field was sprayed with the pesticide or just the area around Aaron's tractor."

"Good point." Jake jotted a note on his pad. "I'll check with the sheriff to see if they took samples in the rest of the field."

Glancing at the wall clock and seeing that it was nearly two thirty, I said, "Back to our list of suspects."

When school got out at three, Dad would need to go on duty in the teen lounge. That meant that I would have to be downstairs dealing with the dime store customers, and I didn't want to miss anything.

"Let's start with Josh Camilo." Jake looked at Quito. "Do you know why Burgess got into it with him at Gossip Central?"

Quito shook his head. "I didn't know that he had. I can't imagine what the problem was between them. I know they were in high school together, but I'm pretty sure they haven't hung out together recently."

Jake's expression didn't show it, but I could tell he was frustrated. I turned slightly to study Quito, who seemed to be telling the truth.

Jake continued, "How about Blake Laudon? We heard that he had a grudge against you both."

I flicked a glance at Boone, and thankfully he

nodded that he'd told Quito about us looking at his phone.

"That's true, but he wouldn't kill Aaron." Quito frowned. "We served together. That's a bond that can't be broken."

It was plain to see that Quito was uncomfortable with the question. But what had he expected? That without prying into the past, Jake would saddle up and ride off to save the day?

"Did you have any contact with Laudon since he parted ways with you and Burgess?" I asked.

"Not really." Quito shook his head. Sincerity dripped from his voice as he explained, "He called, but I never picked up."

"Did he leave a message?" I asked, keeping my tone neutral.

"No."

It seemed odd that Laudon would call but not leave a message. I took a peek at Jake, who dipped his head slightly, indicating we were on the same page.

"Do you think he called Aaron too?" Boone asked.

"Doubtful." Quito shrugged. "He was madder at him than me."

Looking at Jake, Boone said, "I'd like you to start investigating immediately. Do you have a contract for Q to sign, or is the one I signed on his behalf enough?"

"I need some more information before I decide whether to continue with the case." Jake leaned forward and folded his hands on the desktop. "Let's talk about Harry Josephson. Was he trying to buy the farm? Was Aaron resisting?"

"He's been around a couple of times asking if we'd be interested in a deal." Quito huffed, "But killing Aaron wouldn't do much good. Josephson would have to deal with me, and I made it clear that I wasn't selling."

"With Aaron gone" — Boone's voice was gentle — "are you able to handle all the work alone?"

"I'll have to hire some help." Quito took a deep breath. "But this is the first time I owned anything, and I'm never giving it up."

My Spidey senses were tingling. In my prior life, before I bought the dime store, I had worked a lot of years for an investment company. Granted, that business had collapsed when the owner was arrested for fraud, but I had been a damn good financial consultant, which meant being able to read people's motivations. Maybe Quito had gotten rid of Aaron to stop him from selling the farm.

CHAPTER 24
Jake

Jake watched Devereaux walk out of his office doorway. They'd heard the first wave of teenagers arriving downstairs, and her father couldn't handle the kids and after-school shoppers by himself.

Refocusing, he shoved back his chair, opened the desk drawer, and withdrew a single sheet of paper. He glanced at it, then offered it to Quito, who looked at Boone.

"Are you sure we need to do this?" Quito asked. "The sheriff let me go, so maybe they don't even consider me a suspect anymore."

Boone gritted his teeth and said slowly, "Like I told you a few hundred times last night, they let you go because they couldn't hold you without arresting you, which they will do as soon as they find more evidence." He held up his hand before his boyfriend could speak. "And, yes, even though you're innocent, they may well find evidence that still points to you."

"Maybe now that they know what poisoned Aaron, they won't think it was me." Quito's expression was hopeful. "They can ask Dr. Underwood if any of that stuff was on my clothes."

Boone exchanged a glance with Jake, then said, "Which it is likely to be since you carried Aaron from the tractor to your truck and then from your truck to the clinic."

Jake added, "It's possible the sheriff will expand his search, but the fact they weren't concerned about Burgess's wife leaving town and that Kruse was here interviewing Dev and me makes it more likely they are concentrating on you. In my experience, law enforcement generally relies on the bird-in-the-hand theory until proven wrong."

Quito stared at the paper in Jake's hand. "How much will this cost me?"

"It's a standard contract." Jake passed him the document. "You agree to pay an immediate retainer of a thousand dollars. I charge fifty an hour plus expenses. Meetings, travel time, and phone conversations are also billed at that rate, so if you call me for continual updates, it will cost you and annoy the heck out of me."

"I'll leave pestering you to Boone." Quito rolled his eyes at the man by his side. "He's Mr. Impatient, not me. Give me a pen and I'll sign it."

Jake stared at his new client, and instead of handing over the Bic, he warned, "As per section eight of the contract, if you fail to provide me with accurate information, I'm not responsible for unproductive investigative time. I can and will stop the investigation. In addition, any remaining portion of the retainer is forfeited."

"Understood." Quito accepted the pen and scrawled his name, then reached into the pocket of his jeans and took out his wallet. "I hope you take Visa, because my checkbook was burned up in the fire."

Jake nodded. He picked up his cell phone, then attached the device that allowed him to process credit cards. Quito swiped his card, and when the signature line popped up, he scrawled his name on the cell's screen.

Handing the device back to Jake, he asked, "When can you start?"

"Right now." Jake rose to his feet. "Let's head over to Aaron's house. I want to look around and see if there are any clues."

"Is that legal?" Quito frowned.

"Mrs. Burgess gave you the key, so you are authorized to go inside. As long as you invite me in, we're not breaking and entering, so yeah."

"Do I have to be there while you search?" Quito asked. "I have an appointment with the insurance adjuster in half an hour."

Jake smiled to himself, happy he wouldn't have a nervous client looking over his shoulder. "You can unlock the door and invite me inside Aaron's place, then leave for your appointment and come back when you're finished."

"Great." Boone stood. "You can follow us."

Shaking Jake's hand, Quito said, "Thanks for helping."

Jake sent Devereaux a quick message to let her know where he was heading and to tell her that he'd be back by six to take her to dinner. Neither one of them would feel like cooking tonight, and his stomach was not in favor of a repeat of last night's cold cut sandwich supper.

Once he finished texting, he hurried down the stairs, through the storeroom, and into the small parking lot behind the store. After hopping into his truck, he drove through the alley and met up with Boone and Quito on Main Street.

As he followed Boone's Mercedes, on which, evidently, he'd been able to replace the tires, Jake contemplated the case. If Quito was innocent, who was guilty?

The spouse and the best friend were usually the prime suspects, but if they were off the table, next up would be either someone holding a grudge or someone profiting from the vic's death.

He needed to locate and interview Laudon, Josephson, and Camilo. They would be on the top of his to-do list tomorrow once the ranch work was done.

Allowing his mind to wander, Jake's glance fell on the passenger seat. It was there that he'd first kissed Devereaux. Parked beside a frozen pond on a cold February evening, it had felt like they were the only two people in the world.

At that moment, he'd known that she was the woman who was always meant to be in his arms. It had felt better than the first time he made an arrest as a US Marshal.

Jake tightened his grip on the steering wheel as a gust of wind buffeted the high-profile truck. It might have technically been spring, but the gloomy weather reminded him more of fall. Clouds rolled across the ashen sky and rain threatened the horizon.

As he made the turn onto the county road, the smooth pavement changed into patched blacktop. A few minutes later, the blinker on Boone's car came on, and Jake followed the Mercedes into a driveway covered in white pea gravel.

The house was the typical gray-shingled, two-story home found around rural Missouri. It was probably about eighteen hundred square feet with an attached garage and a porch that stretched across the front.

In the rear of the property, there was a metal building that doubtlessly contained farm equipment. Jake made a mental note to take a look inside before he left.

Quito hopped from Boone's car, jogged up the sidewalk, and unlocked the front door. Jake watched as he knelt to pet the border collie that greeted him. Once the canine was under control, Jake joined the pair in the small foyer.

Quito swept his hand across the dog's head and said, "I'll take Trooper to Boone's. He'd be lonely here all by himself, so he might as well stay with us until Rose gets home." He stared at Jake and added, "I'll be back as soon as I can. Don't mess anything up."

"No one will ever be able to tell that I was even here," Jake assured him.

He grinned to himself. Boone was getting quite a menagerie at his place. First, he'd adopted a cat who had been left orphaned when his owner had been murdered, then Escobar and his dog moved in, and now the Burgess canine. For someone as fussy as the elegant attorney, all the shedding and various animal accessories scattered around must be driving Boone crazy.

Chuckling, Jake watched Quito leave with Trooper, then walked down a hallway that ended in a combination of dining area, kitchen, and family room. The space was immaculate. There wasn't even a trace that anyone lived there.

Stepping farther into the open expanse, Jake started opening drawers and cabinets. He wasn't sure what he was looking for but would know it if he saw it.

After searching every nook and cranny and coming up with nothing more interesting than a spare light for the refrigerator and a roll of stamps, Jake took a seat at the kitchen table. He made a detailed sketch of the area, then got up and headed down a second corridor.

He ended up in the formal living room. The walls were covered in poster-sized pictures of Rose Burgess. Jake recognized the stunning woman from the headshots Devereaux had printed off of her social media account.

He inspected the photos, noting the exotic locations and expensive clothing and jewelry. Obviously, these were all from Rose's modeling career.

Jake made another sketch, then took the stairs to the second floor. There were three bedrooms. One was clearly a guest room, another the master bedroom, and the third an office.

Jake searched the guest room and master. There was nothing in either one that gave him any kind of clue as to who Aaron Burgess was or why anyone might want him dead.

All the drawers in the desk and file cabinet were locked, but Jake made quick work of picking them. He found mostly farm records and household bills, all in folders with neatly printed labels.

Jake snapped photos of the paperwork from the past year. There didn't seem to be much beyond utilities, tax records, and various credit card statements, but he'd show everything to Devereaux. She was the financial whiz and would spot anything fishy a lot faster than he would.

Once he was finished with the files, he looked around for a computer or tablet. There wasn't anything like that in sight, but there was a charger lying on the desk. It was connected to an electrical socket as if someone had taken whatever it was meant to serve.

Jake figured Rose was traveling with whichever device normally resided on the desktop. He rechecked the room for a thumb drive but didn't find one.

Disappointed, he carefully relocked all the drawers, then headed downstairs and into the garage. It contained a riding lawnmower and tools hanging from a pegboard above a workbench. One vehicle spot was empty, but a beat-up pickup truck occupied the other side—Burgess had probably walked back to the equipment shed and driven the tractor to the field.

Jake clenched his jaw. He hadn't found anything unusual or anything that had given him a lead to follow. As soon as his client returned and locked up, he'd take a ride past the crime scene and see if the sheriff had it taped off.

If so, he'd text Kruse and ask if the area away from the tractor had any trace of malathion. If the area hadn't been tested, at least Jake's message might nudge the sheriff into doing so. Kruse had seemed like an okay guy who would be willing to share information and take suggestions.

Jake glanced at his watch. It was five thirty. Quito and Boone had been gone ninety minutes and so should be coming back soon. While he waited, he'd check out the metal building at the rear of the property.

Walking outside, the wind felt colder than before, and a few raindrops fell on his face, but Jake was still smiling. He was really glad he'd gotten a PI license and happy that Devereaux had gotten hers too.

Jake enjoyed ranching, but the thrill of being on a case was hard to beat. He briefly wondered if Meg missed the thrill of the chase or if she was happy with her safe, but dull, job working at Underwood's clinic.

She'd originally claimed that she needed something to do until she was strong enough to go back to the marshal service. But she'd shown no signs of returning to St. Louis. Maybe her lover's death would be the impetus she needed to leave Shadow Bend.

Jake didn't trust his ex and figured she had to have some reason for taking that job and for sticking around. He just couldn't figure out what.

Which reminded him, he needed to check out the motel Meg and Burgess were using for their affair. Maybe it hadn't been as big a secret as the lovebirds thought.

CHAPTER 25
Devereaux

I was finishing up the final touches on the bachelorette basket when Jake strolled into the store. The teen lounge officially shut down at five, and my father had left a few minutes later, right after the last kid had disappeared.

Because Shadow Bend still operated on a farming/ranching schedule, meals for most of the town's original citizens were promptly at six, noon, and five thirty. Which meant it was rare to have a customer after the teens went home, and I generally used that time for bookkeeping.

The newcomers or country clubbers, as many old-timers called them, ate to their own dinner bell, but most of them commuted back from Kansas City and didn't get into town until well after six thirty. By then, the dime store had been locked up for half an hour, and I was already walking in my front door.

Making a woeful face at Jake, I said, "I'm famished."

I'd only make that type of statement if I was sure there were no customers present. Not only did I worry about being judged unprofessional, but with my curvier than acceptable figure, I also didn't want anyone thinking that I should lose weight. It wasn't going to happen—I had long since resigned myself to the fact that while brain cells might die, fat cells lived forever—and a snide comment from a shopper might result in a snarky comeback.

Jake chuckled at my pitiful expression. "We can't have that." He turned around, locked the entrance, and flipped the open sign to read CLOSED.

"Where are we going for dinner?" I asked, my stomach rumbling.

Facing me again, he tilted his head thoughtfully. "How does Chinese sound?"

"Perfect." I hurriedly covered the basket and walked around the counter. "Boone, Quito, and Poppy want to join us. Is that okay?"

Jake blew out a sigh. "I was hoping to have you to myself, but I suppose everyone wants an update."

"Yep."

I gave him a kiss that promised more later, then sent a quick text to Poppy and Boone telling them to meet us at the Golden Dragon.

Without waiting for a reply from my friends, I headed toward the storage room and took off my Devereaux's Dime Store sweatshirt. As I pulled a baby-blue sweater over my head, I raised my voice so

Jake could hear me through the knit fabric. "It'll be easier to give them a report all at once and not have them all bugging you individually."

"There's not much to tell." Jake's response was muffled by the sweater.

As soon as my face emerged from the sweater, I grabbed my purse and said, "Then it's even more efficient to inform them of that as a group rather than answer three individual calls."

Jake nodded and followed me out the back door. I paused to lock up, and when I finished, he already had the truck backed out of his parking spot and aimed toward the alley.

I hopped into the running pickup and used the short ride over to fix my hair. A few minutes later, I glanced away from the sun visor mirror just as Jake turned into the restaurant's entrance.

Shoot! The lot was packed. Was everyone in town having supper here?

Jake drove up and down the aisles until I spied a car pulling out. I pointed to the opening, and he whipped the truck into the slot. He just beat a Land Rover Defender trying for the same spot, and the driver, a bearded guy wearing a knit beanie like a snood and retro wire-rim glasses, gave us the finger.

Jake shook his head. "I thought that hipsters were supposed to be so mellow."

"What?" I giggled. "You don't appreciate how much pain you have to endure to be on the cutting edge?"

Chuckling, we strolled toward the restaurant. Every time we ate here, I marveled that up until a couple of years ago the building had been a house of worship. When the Methodists had put up a new church near the highway, they sold their old structure. The current owners had renovated the interior but left the exterior pretty much as it had been when the place was first built.

My stomach was unhappy to see that the line for a table extended all the way out to the sidewalk. At this rate, I wouldn't get my hot and sour soup for another hour.

Happily, before we joined the queue, I heard Poppy's voice yelling our name.

She was standing inside the doorway, gesturing for us to come in. With murmured apologies as we passed up the folks standing in line, we joined her in the lobby.

The smells of ginger, soy sauce, and sesame oil greeted us when we stepped over the threshold, and as I took a huge whiff, I almost missed Poppy's words. "Noah had that huge table in back to himself and asked us to sit with him. I hope you don't mind."

Jake and I exchanged startled glances, and I quickly said, "That could be awkward."

"Noah's fine with it." Poppy's smooth forehead wrinkled, then her eyes widened. "You and he aren't still dancing around each other, are you?"

"Of course not." I blew out an exasperated

breath. "I've told you a million times, Noah understands that what he and I had was just a leftover crush from our teenage years." When Poppy only raised an eyebrow, I explained, "The awkwardness is because Jake dumped Noah as a client in order to work for Quito."

"Oh." Poppy's cupid's bow lips formed a perfect circle.

I lowered my voice. "Also, we thought we'd bring you all up to date on the case over dinner."

"Well, that's fine then." Poppy grinned. "Quito has already filled in Noah on what's happened, so clearly he doesn't care if you share in front of him."

Jake shot a look at the people in line behind us, most of whom weren't even trying to hide that they were eavesdropping. "Fine, let's just sit down before everyone in Shadow Bend is in the know."

With a nod of agreement, Poppy started to lead the way, but the hostess, a stunning Asian woman in her early twenties, glided between us and said, "I'm sorry, but you'll need to leave your name and join the queue." She glanced at the tablet she held and asked, "Smoking or nonsmoking?"

Whispering in Jake's ear, I said, "Isn't that like asking peeing or non-peeing section in a swimming pool?"

While I was being witty, Poppy said, "We're with Dr. Underwood's party."

Without waiting for the hostess to acknowledge her statement, she tried to step around the woman.

The hostess moved to block her and thrust out her arm.

"He didn't mention that anyone was joining him." The hostess smoothed her gorgeous yellow silk dress over her slim hips. "So many ladies claim to be with the doctor. One moment while I check with him."

Jake frowned at Poppy. "I thought you said that you, Boone, and Quito were already sitting with Underwood?"

"The Empress of the Universe must not have noticed us when we first arrived." Poppy glared at the hostess's retreating figure. "I can't believe that woman thinks she has to protect him."

"Everyone in town protects him." Just in case Jake was feeling a bit insecure with the situation, I looped my arm through his and hugged it to my side. "Noah has it all—money, good looks, social position. And don't forget he's the town's beloved doctor."

The hostess returned before either Poppy or Jake could respond to my statement and said, "Please follow me."

"I know my way," Poppy objected, but either the hostess didn't hear her or ignored her because the woman stuck out her chest, which was clearly exhibited by the deep V of the sheath's neckline, and continued to escort us to a large table set apart from the others.

As we trailed her, Poppy muttered, "What is this? Bring your breasts to work day? When did the uniforms here go from a mandarin collar to a display case?"

Jake chuckled then murmured into my ear, "This should be interesting."

"You're right. But since it's in the back and partly obscured by that lacquer screen, Noah's table is the best one in the house if we don't want to be overheard."

As we approached, Noah sprang to his feet and greeted us, then motioned for us to sit. I quickly slid onto the bench on one side of the booth and Jake joined me. Boone and Quito were on the other bench facing us, which left Poppy and Noah. Poppy took the empty seat next to Jake, and Noah took the one beside Boone.

When the six of us were settled, the hostess handed us large red leather folders. She stood there for a second, then when it was clear that Noah's attention was focused on Poppy, she reluctantly departed.

As with many Chinese restaurants, the menus were multi-paged. My stomach growled as I considered the choices.

Jake nudged me and proposed, "Let's order enough so we have leftovers to take home."

"That sounds good to me," I said, then looked around the table and asked, "What's everyone else having?"

Boone took Quito's hand. "We're sharing a sesame chicken with a large order of fried rice."

"My usual mo po tofu," Poppy answered.

"Beef and broccoli for me," Noah said, then suggested, "How about a couple of orders of pot stickers to share?"

"Yes." Poppy clapped. "Hot and sour soup too."

Our server magically appeared as soon as we all closed our menus, and after we conveyed our choices, she ascertained that we weren't ordering drinks, then poured us each a cup of tea and left.

Once she was out of earshot, Boone pointed at Jake and said, "So, tell us what you found at the Burgess residence."

"Is that okay with you, Quito?" Jake asked.

"Yes. I know you all are trying to help me."

Jake looked across the table at Noah and said, "No hard feelings, Doc. I just figured Quito had more at stake in the situation than you, so I ought to be working for him."

"I agree." Noah leaned forward to see Quito around Boone and said, "But I'd be happy to help with the cost."

"That's mighty nice of you, Dr. Underwood." Quito gave Noah an appreciative nod. "But it's covered."

Jake summarized what we had learned leading up to his visit to the Burgess house, then said, "There wasn't anything there that stood out, but I did take pictures of the financial paperwork." He tapped my arm. "Devereaux is much better at interpreting that sort of thing than me, so I wanted her to take a look and see if there were red flags of any sort."

"Sure." Warmth spread through me at the knowledge that Jake really did see me as a useful part of his investigative team. "I'll load it into some software that I have. It'll set off an alarm if something doesn't seem right."

"There wasn't anything else?" Boone questioned.

"Unfortunately, there was no computer." Jake sighed. "I was really hoping to get a copy of the hard drive. That's where people's real secrets pop up." He looked at Quito. "Do you know if the Burgesses have one?"

"Aaron used his phone for e-mail and the internet." Quito tapped his fingers on the tabletop. "Rose acted as our bookkeeper, and I know she has a laptop. She probably has it with her."

While everyone chimed in on what might be on the absent device, I realized what had been bothering me, and when there was a lull in the conversation, I asked, "Noah, where's Meg?"

"She's in St. Louis." Noah's expression was difficult to read.

"Something to do with the marshals?" I asked, hoping that she was returning to her old job and moving away from Shadow Bend.

Poppy must have been on the same wavelength, because she said, "Yeah. She seems fine now and her disability leave must be about up."

"I'm not sure." Noah paused while our soup was

served, then when the server left, he continued, "She didn't say and I didn't ask."

"Really?" I murmured.

"We're not dating anymore." Noah concentrated on dipping his spoon into the rich soup, but I noticed he sneaked a glance at Poppy. "There wasn't any spark, so we're back to her just working at the clinic."

Poppy didn't quite succeed in keeping the grin off her face. "Probably for the best."

I felt Jake looking at me and turned my head. When our gazes met, he raised a brow and I nodded.

Doubtlessly we were both thinking the same thing. Had Meg decided to call it quits with Noah because she knew that there was no way to keep her affair with Aaron quiet?

Having the whole town know that she had slept with another woman's husband, then been dumped by the beloved town doctor, would not be a pleasant experience. It might make a person like Meg face some unpleasant truths about herself. And her narcissistic tendencies wouldn't handle that well at all.

Yes. I had labeled Meg without being a licensed psychiatrist. But after years in the cutthroat world of finance, narcissism was one disorder that I was qualified to diagnose without attending med school.

Meg ticked nearly all the boxes. She felt entitled to have whatever she wanted—even if it, or he, belonged to someone else. She had no qualms in exploiting people to get her own way. She was a bully of the worst sort, enjoying the belittlement of other women.

And the most telling sign, she required constant admiration. Especially by the male of the species.

Hmm! Maybe Aaron had tried to break up with Meg, and she was the mastermind behind his death.

Surely, an experienced marshal would be able to figure out a way to poison the guy while appearing to have an ironclad alibi.

CHAPTER 26
Devereaux

If my suspicions about Meg were true, we needed to know her whereabouts. I waited for Jake to come to the same conclusion, but he continued to eat his soup without any visible sign that he and I were on the same page.

I cleared my throat and stared at him, but he didn't take the hint. Evidently, unlike me, he still didn't consider his ex a suspect.

Sniffing at his obtuseness, I resolved to wait until we were alone to suggest that she should be on our list. I probably wouldn't point out that Jake should have thought of her himself.

Then again, I might drop just the tiniest hint. You know, just to keep him on his toes.

In the meantime, I decided to see if her alibi was as solid as it seemed, so I looked at Noah and asked, "Was Meg at the clinic the whole time you were open on Saturday?"

"Yes," Noah confirmed. "We had a full schedule, so we even had to have sandwiches delivered for lunch. Usually, Meg would go pick them up, but I just couldn't spare her that day."

"Why do you care about Meg's work schedule?" Poppy gave me a confused look.

Remembering my promise to keep Meg and the victim's affair quiet, I quickly lied, "Just wondering if she was present when Quito brought in Aaron."

Poppy opened her mouth, clearly skeptical of my explanation, but before she could speak, the server approached the table and put down two platters of pot stickers.

Once the waitress was gone and we'd all helped ourselves to the appetizers, Jake said, "Doc, did the sheriff ever get in touch with you?"

"He stopped by my house this morning," Noah affirmed. "He told me that Mr. Burgess was poisoned by the inhalation of malathion."

"Did he say how Aaron was contaminated with the toxin?" I put a dumpling on my plate, used my fork to break it in half, then chewed thoughtfully. "He was pretty cagey when he told us about it." Glancing at Jake, I added, "We don't believe for a minute Aaron would sit still while someone approached him and sprayed him with the stuff."

"You're right." Quito nodded. "And when I found him, he was just sitting on the tractor. It didn't look as if he had attempted to run away or chase anyone."

"Any idea how fast malathion would disable an average-sized healthy male, Doc?" Jake asked.

"It would depend on the level of exposure." Noah pointed his chopsticks at Jake and lectured, "I did some research, and the median lethal dose of malathion is estimated to be twenty-one hundred milligrams per kilogram in mammals."

"Which I'm guessing is a lot higher than you'd get in any kind of accidental contact," Jake responded.

Noah nodded, then paused while the waitress cleared our used plates and distributed clean dishes for our entrees. She returned a few seconds later with our main courses.

Once we had all helped ourselves, Noah said, "Malathion overwhelms the nervous system. By switching on junctions that then cannot be turned off, the toxin causes the nerves to fire excessively. Eventually, the lungs fill with fluid and the person stops breathing."

Boone sighed. "That still leaves a lot of questions, especially how someone managed to spray Aaron without alarming him. If he felt threatened, surely he would have gotten off the tractor and tried to escape."

"Unless he didn't see it coming." Quito shook his head. "But I can't think of a scenario where a person could approach Aaron in an open field without being noticed."

We all agreed, then another random thought surfaced in my overcrowded brain, and I said, "Boone, where was Tsar last Saturday? He wasn't at your house when I checked inside to see if you were okay."

"I had asked my parents to take care of him." Boone smiled fondly. "I expected to be away for at least twenty-four hours and didn't want him to be alone. Mom loves him almost more than I do and was happy to cat sit."

"I thought your folks didn't know about you and Quito?" Poppy's nose twitched as she scented an inconsistency in Boone's story.

Boone rolled his eyes at her distrustful nature. "They were under the impression that I was going into Kansas City to meet some friends and see a show, not to have a romantic tryst."

"Come to think of it," I said slowly, "what about your tires? Any idea who slashed them?"

Boone shook his head. "I discovered the vandalism when I was leaving to go into the city for my date with Quito." Noah exchanged a fond look with his boyfriend. "Since I didn't want to be late, I walked over to my parents' and borrowed their car. With all that's going on, I never did report the damage to the police."

"Dad's aware of it," Poppy said, then added, "But he probably is waiting for a formal complaint before proceeding."

"I'll do that tomorrow so I can put in an insurance claim." Boone shrugged. "But I doubt the cops will find the culprit. It was probably some random teenager. I must have forgotten to engage the deadbolt when I got home that afternoon, a mistake I won't make again. There's been a lot of little nuisance crimes on our street lately and I should have been more careful. I sure made sure it was locked before I left for the city."

"You don't think there's a connection between your slashed tires, Aaron, and Quito's house being burned down?" I asked, trying to see a broader picture.

"No one knew Quito and I were seeing each other," Boone protested.

"Hmm." Here was another person who thought their romance could be kept a secret.

I glanced at Jake and he nodded his agreement. It was reassuring that he'd be on the alert for any possible connections. I let the subject drop and turned my attention to dinner.

While we all ate, we kept the conversation to everyday subjects and avoided the topic of Shadow Bend's recent spate of criminal activity. Instead, we discussed how our families were doing, the scavenger hunt that the city council had planned in the town square for May Day, and the colder than usual weather.

Still, when the server brought our check and a fistful of fortune cookies, I wondered if the universe would give us any hints that might help us find Aaron's killer. I waited until everyone had made their selection, then I picked up the one that remained.

Whatever machine had wrapped my cookie hadn't been functioning correctly. It must have been set to dispense an excess of adhesive, and I struggled to open the little cellophane envelope.

Finally, I gave the edges a mighty tug. Instead of parting smoothly as I had expected, the entire package erupted in a shower of brittle tan crumbs.

Boone arched an eyebrow and commented, "You know it's never a good sign when your fortune cookie explodes."

As we all agreed, Poppy pushed away her empty dish and said, "With that ominous pronouncement, I need a potty break."

As soon as she left, Noah stood up and said, "May I speak to you alone, Dev?"

Ignoring Jake's unhappy growl, I nodded and got to my feet. Noah led me into an empty room that the restaurant rented out for parties and closed the door.

He swallowed a few times, then cleared his throat and, looking somewhere over my shoulder, asked, "Is Poppy seeing anyone?"

"No." I shook my head. "I think Tryg was the last guy she dated, and that's been over for a while." I didn't allow my pleased expression to show and instead continued, "She's super picky and past the stage of casual flings."

"So, you think she's ready to settle down?" Noah fiddled with a pen in his shirt pocket.

"Definitely." I put my hand over his to still his fingers. "She was never as wild as her reputation made her out to be. A lot of that was just to tick off her father."

"Has she ever indicated that she might, uh…" Noah shot me a hopeful look and trailed off.

"Without betraying any confidences," I started, thinking fast, "there is someone that she likes, but for various reasons, she feels like she can't initiate the relationship."

"Reasons like he was once involved with her best friend?" Noah asked.

"That." I nodded. "And because he then quickly started dating someone else."

"That was a bad rebound decision," Noah admitted. "Meg set her sights on me. I should have resisted, but my ego was pretty beat up at the time, so I didn't."

"Pushing all that aside…" I really didn't want to go into how I had hurt Noah. We'd hashed it out enough times, and repeating the same conversation wouldn't help either of us move past it. "What are you going to do about Poppy now?"

"I'll ask her out." Noah nodded to himself. "I'll make sure we both are the last to leave and ask her then."

I pointed a finger at him. "Make sure you do." We headed back to our table, but just before we were in earshot of the others, I said, "I'd better get a squealing phone call from Poppy within the next couple of hours or I'll get ahold of Meg and tell her you're sorry you two broke up and want her back."

"Not that!" Noah raised his hands in surrender. "I swear I'll ask Poppy tonight if she'll go out with me."

CHAPTER 27
Jake

Jake had slept poorly. The pain in his leg and thoughts of the Burgess murder kept him awake as he alternated between staring at the ceiling and the clock.

He was afraid that he would disturb Devereaux with his tossing and turning, so around three a.m., he gave up and got out of bed. After settling into the recliner with a heating pad and a clipboard, he started a list of who he wanted to interview and what information he needed to gather.

A couple of hours later, he woke up with a start and squinted at the wall clock. It was a little after five. Time to get his ass in gear and start the morning chores.

He walked quietly into the bedroom, dressed, then went outside. It looked as if the weather would be a repeat of the past couple of days—cold, windy, and with just enough rain to be annoying.

Although it was technically spring, the grass was

still sparse, and the cows needed to have supplemental hay delivered to the pastures. While he and the hands hauled bail after bail, Jake considered the rest of his day.

Devereaux had to work at the dime store, so he'd be on his own until six. He'd use that time to talk to the people he thought would respond better to him without her along. She'd be disappointed, but he'd bring her up to speed over supper. Maybe they'd finally get to have dinner alone.

A few hours later, when Jake strolled into the house for breakfast, Devereaux was sitting at the kitchen table, sipping a cup of coffee, and looking at the local paper. She was dressed in her usual work uniform—jeans and a dime store sweatshirt—this one was a soft peach. She had her pretty red gold hair in some fancy kind of braid over her shoulder, and she played with the ends as she read.

"Mornin', sugar," Jake drawled, dropping a kiss on her upturned lips. "Sleep well?"

"Better than you." She shot him a knowing looking, got up, and walked to the stove. "Anything wrong?"

"Just the Burgess case running through my head." Jake deliberately didn't mention his leg, or she'd bug him to let the doctor know that he was still experiencing quite a bit of pain from his injury.

"Right." Her response was skeptical. "I made oatmeal and sausages."

"Perfect." Jake rummaged through the pantry,

pulling out a bag of brown sugar, a container of walnuts, and another of dried cranberries.

By the time he had gathered the fixings, Devereaux had steaming bowls of oatmeal at each of their places and a sizzling platter of sausages in the middle of the table.

He poured himself a cup of coffee and topped off Devereaux's mug, then took the chair opposite hers. It was a little disconcerting seeing her in Tony's usual spot, and Jake briefly wondered if his uncle was sitting in Dev's seat over at Birdie's house.

He grinned to himself, thinking about Tony finally living with his first love. He hoped the octogenarian couple would have many years together. He also hoped they didn't drive each other crazy, since both his uncle and Birdie usually had a strong opinion about everything, and neither of them was shy about sharing it.

While he and Devereaux piled toppings onto their oatmeal, he said, "After I finish here, I'll try and track down the army buddy and the real estate guy. What do you have going at the store today?"

"I've got two groups coming in." Devereaux rolled her eyes. "Since the Knittie Gritties had to cancel yesterday because of some sort of yarn emergency, they're meeting this afternoon, and Scrapbooking Scalawags are scheduled for this morning." She took a bite of her breakfast, swallowed, and added, "It's too bad that it wasn't the Quilting

Queens' week, because then I could just leave up the tables."

Jake nodded his understanding. In exchange for craft groups buying the materials for their projects from the dime store, Devereaux provided them with a meeting space. A bonus was that they also purchased refreshments and usually any odds and ends that also caught their eye.

Devereaux had fashioned a crafting alcove in the rear of the building. For the knitters, crocheters, and needlepointers, she hauled out the comfy chairs and ottomans from the storeroom, while the scrapbookers, quilters, and sewers required long worktables. Each group was a lot of work, and Devereaux would be managing it all alone today until Taryn showed up after school let out.

As Jake considered his fiancée's workload, he shoveled oatmeal into his mouth. He was always starving when he came in from doing morning chores.

Quickly finished with his first bowl, he refilled it from the pan on the stove, then said, "I can come in around noon and help you switch out the furniture in the alcove."

"No. You need to investigate the murder." Devereaux ate a sausage link. "If it's too much for me, I'll call Dad and ask him to lend me some muscle."

"Call if you change your mind." Jake picked up the newspaper Dev had been reading. "Anything about the murder in here?"

"Nothing. But this is local. We need to look at the

county paper." Devereaux made a face. "I checked the obituaries, which by the way would be a lot more interesting if they told you how the person died, but Aaron wasn't listed."

"Ha ha." Jake shook his head. Devereaux always managed to surprise him with her quirky sense of humor.

She tapped his empty mug. "Want a refill?"

"Sure." Jake rubbed his hands together. "Hard to warm up after being outside on a day like today. It's colder than the mayor's heart."

"Yeah. Speaking of Hizzoner, did you know he's running again?" Devereaux grabbed his cup. "Politicians should be limited to two terms. One in office and one in prison."

Jake chuckled his agreement, then asked, "Any idea where I can find Josephson?"

"He has a real estate office in town." Devereaux finished fixing Jake's coffee and sat back down. "Do you know where the other guy lives?"

"I asked Quito, and he said that last he heard, Laudon was in Chicago." Jake shrugged. "I'll try calling him to get his current location."

"How will you ask him?" A crease appeared between Devereaux's beautiful blue-green eyes.

"I'll wing it." Jake settled more comfortably into the wooden slat-back chair. "Probably start out with asking him why he's been trying to get in touch with Quito."

"Hmm." Devereaux's expression was thoughtful. "Maybe intimate that Quito and Aaron aren't getting along in their partnership and are looking to split up." She quirked her mouth. "That might tickle his fancy."

"That's a good suggestion." Jake took a small notebook from the back pocket of his jeans. "What do you know about the real estate guy?"

"As Walter Kerr said, Josephson has delusions of adequacy. He doesn't have the best reputation." Devereaux started to clear the table. "He's the man you go to if you want your property sold no questions asked. He's always got some kind of sleezy scheme going on under the table." As she rinsed the dirty dishes and put them in the dishwasher, she added, "He's pals with the mayor."

Jake snorted. "Well, that says it all." He rose to his feet and began putting away the containers he'd taken from the pantry, then followed Devereaux's glance as she looked at the wall clock. She had to leave soon. "Let's plan on going out to dinner—alone." He emphasized the word. "I'll pick you up at the store at six."

"Okay." Devereaux dried her hands, leaned into him for a kiss, then walked away. Just before she disappeared down the hall, she paused and said, "Shoot, I almost forgot. You left your cell phone on the nightstand, and it's been ringing all morning."

"Was it the same person calling?" Jake trailed her as she headed into the bedroom.

"I didn't look." Devereaux kept going into the

master bath, and when Jake caught up, she was putting on lip gloss. Once she was finished, she added, "I didn't want to be nosy."

Jake grinned, already planning on smearing the pretty pink gloss she'd just applied. "I have nothing to hide. Feel free to look through my phone any time."

"I thought it might be Meg," Devereaux admitted, not looking at him.

"Even more reason for you to answer it." Jake winked. "That would drive her plumb crazy since I always hid my phone from her."

Devereaux chuckled, then frowned. "So why can I look at it?"

Jake clenched his jaw, hating the memories of his time with his ex. "Because things are different with us, and I want to keep it that way."

"We trust each other." Devereaux's eyes softened. "And you never trusted her."

Jake froze. She was right. Even when they were first together, he hadn't completely trusted Meg. And the feeling was mutual. Why had he been such a fool to marry her?

As Devereaux fussed with her hair, Jake checked his phone. There were three hang-ups from an unknown number and a text from that same number that turned out being from his ex.

He felt Devereaux's gaze on him while he was reading it and held it up for her to see.

STAYING IN ST. LOUIS. I HIRED A COMPANY

TO PACK UP MY STUFF AND MOVE IT NORTH. IT'S BEEN FUN, BUT IT'S TIME TO GET BACK TO MY REAL LIFE.

She'd signed it with a kissy-face emoji.

Jake raised his eyes from the screen, not sure what to expect from Devereaux.

Her expression was hard to read, and there was an overly long pause before she said, "Do you think there's any chance Meg killed Aaron?"

Jake hadn't been expecting that and questioned, "What makes you ask that?"

"Here's the thing." Devereaux bit her lip, then described her theory about Meg's narcissism.

Jake frowned as he considered Devereaux's explanation. "Those are all valid points," Jake agreed.

"I know Meg has an alibi," Devereaux continued, "but she probably also has methods that regular, non-marshal folks don't."

CHAPTER 28
Jake

Jake watched Devereaux's car disappear around the curve as she headed down the lane, then he hurried away to finish his chores. It was strange. They'd only been living together for three days, and already the ranch felt empty when she was gone.

He shook his head. He'd never expected to feel this way, but she'd become his whole world.

The rest of the morning passed in a whirl of activity, and it was already half past noon when he gave the ranch hands instructions for the rest of the day. By one, Jake had showered, dressed, and hopped into his truck.

Before pulling out onto the road, Jake paused to call Burgess's ex-army buddy. Laudon was on the top of Jake's suspect list, and if he could arrange a meeting, that would be his first priority. If not, he'd head to Josephson's real estate office.

Grabbing his cell from the cup holder, Jake dialed

the number he'd gotten from Quito. While he waited for the call to be answered, he dug out a notepad and pen from the glove box.

The phone rang several times, and Jake was about to hang up when a raspy voice said, "This better not be no telemarketer."

Jake introduced himself as a private investigator working for Quito Escobar and said, "Mr. Escobar who would like to know why you've been phoning him."

"He hired a gumshoe for that?" Laudon's tone was incredulous. "He must have money to burn."

Jake noted the word *burn*. Had that been just an expression or a sly reference to Quito's home being set on fire?

"I can't discuss my client's assets." Jake jotted a note to himself to check with McCall regarding the arson investigation. "Were you calling Mr. Escobar about a financial matter?"

"No." Laudon cleared his throat. "We're old army buddies, and since I was going to be in Kansas City for a while, I was just wanting to see if he'd feel like getting together."

"It's my understanding that you and Mr. Escobar had a falling-out."

"Yeah" — Laudon hesitated — "I regretted that and hoped we could let bygones be bygones."

"Okay." Jake decided to see if he could get Laudon to meet with him in person. "How about this? Since you're in the area, why don't you come into my office this afternoon? I'll arrange for Mr. Escobar to be there, and we'll try to sort this all out."

"Why won't Quito just meet with me by himself?" Laudon demanded.

"After the threats you made, he'd feel more comfortable with a witness."

It was a risk on Jake's part. Quito hadn't mentioned threats. However, he had enough experience to figure out that Laudon hadn't controlled his temper during that last confrontation.

"Well, I suppose that I can understand that," Laudon muttered. "But Quito had to know that I didn't mean what I said. I'd never hurt him."

"So, can you be in Shadow Bend around three?" Jake wanted to get a commitment and to hang up before the man reconsidered or asked more questions.

"Make it four. I just woke up and I need to eat before driving down." Laudon added, "But I don't want to come to your office."

"Why is that?"

"Let's just say that neutral ground works better for me. Hold on a sec." There was a lengthy pause, then Laudon came back on the line and said, "I just booked a room at the Shadow Bend B and B. The owner tells me we can use her parlor to talk."

"Fine," Jake agreed, then quickly disconnected before Laudon changed his mind about meeting.

Putting the truck into gear, he turned in the direction of town. Although he had no intention of arranging for Quito to be present at the interview with Laudon, he would give his client a report afterwards.

There was plenty of time before the Laudon meeting to speak to Josephson, and as Jake drove toward the guy's office, he kept to the speed limit. This gave him a chance to collect his thoughts and figure out a strategy for approaching the real estate mogul.

He'd never met Harry Josephson and wasn't sure what level of cooperation he could expect. However, considering that Devereux had called him sleezy, it was a sure bet that his version of reality might not be the truth.

Even going a sedate fifty-five, his F250 ate up the miles into Shadow Bend and he arrived at one thirty. As Jake crossed the sidewalk, he noticed a Be Back Later sign in the real estate office window.

He started to leave. However before he completely turned away, he saw that the last person hadn't pulled the door totally closed, and Jake pushed it open.

Entering, he noted that the real estate agency was typical for a small town. There were several workspaces containing a desk and chair, as well as a door in the rear that Jake assumed was Josephson's private office.

The cubicles were empty, but a teenager was near a cluster of file cabinets that lined the back wall. She was feeding stacks of paper from the open drawers into a shredder. As she worked, her head bopped to whatever she was listening to via her earbuds.

Jake didn't want to scare the girl, so he cleared his throat. But between the noise of the shredder and her music, she was totally oblivious.

Stepping closer, he raised his voice and said, "Excuse me."

The girl jumped as if he'd thrown a bucket of water on her, then clutched her chest and gasped, "Oh, my gosh. You scared the crap out of me."

"Sorry." Jake bit back a lecture about being more aware of one's surroundings. "Is Mr. Josephson around?"

Narrowing her eyes, the girl asked, "What do you want with him?"

"This is his business," Jake pointed out. "What do most people want with him?"

"You looking to buy a house?" The teenager leaned a slim hip on the open drawer of a file cabinet. "Or are you selling?"

"How about I discuss that with Mr. Josephson?" Jake wondered why the girl was so suspicious.

The teenager peered at him for a long moment, then demanded, "Who shall I say is asking for him?"

"Jake Del Vecchio." He held out his palm. "And you?"

The teenager tentatively shook Jake's hand and muttered, "I'm Ashley Josephson."

"Good to meet you, Ashley." Jake smiled. "Is Harry your father?"

"Yeah." Ashley couldn't have been more than fifteen. "You got a problem with that?"

Jake considered the question. "Why would I?" Something was off here.

The girl wore a pink hoodie with a pair of jeans ripped at the knees and red Converse ankle sneakers. Various-size gold hoops marched up her earlobe, and her long, wavy brown hair had a swath of purple.

Jake frowned. He wouldn't allow his teenage daughter to dress like that.

"Dad is busy, so why don't you come back later." Ashley flicked her fingers at Jake as if she were getting rid of some lint.

Her attitude was annoying, but Jake kept his expression neutral when he said, "Let's allow your father to tell me that himself."

Ashley opened her mouth, then after staring at Jake's unsmiling face, she seemed to reconsider and said, "Fine." She turned toward the closed door in the rear and bellowed, "Dad, some big guy wants to see you."

A few seconds later, the door opened and a stick-thin sixty-something man with a head of white hair took half a step over the threshold. His faded blue eyes were wary, and he tugged at the collar of his white shirt.

"What can I do for you?" He stood well back from Jake, as if poised to flee.

Jake told him his name, then stuck out his hand, but the guy ignored the gesture. He continued to keep his distance and eye Jake as if he were a skunk about to lift his tail.

Barely stopping himself from an eyeroll, Jake maintained his professional demeanor and asked, "Do you have a couple of minutes? I'd like to speak to you about the farmland package you've been putting together."

Josephson tensed. "What about it?"

Jake took a step closer and Josephson shuffled backward until he was once again inside his office. Was this guy expecting someone to come beat him up?

As Josephson attempted to close the door, Jake quickly shoved his foot in the way and said, "I'm interested in the Burgess property."

Josephson blew out what looked like a relieved breath. "I don't represent that acreage."

"But you approached Burgess, right?" Jake kept his boot where it was, afraid the man might still lock himself inside the tiny room.

"I did." Josephson crossed his arms. "But the owners refused."

Jake's voice dripped with skepticism. "And you didn't pursue it?"

"I was going to, and given enough time and incentive, I could have persuaded them to sign with me," Josephson's voice squeaked. "Unfortunately, the corporation I was representing pulled out before I could make that happen. Thus, there is no longer any profit in acquiring that property."

"Why did the company drop the project?" Jake asked, then glanced at Ashley, who had returned to her shredding. "Was there a problem? A legal problem? Like you leaning on property owners to sell?"

"Of course not!" Josephson jabbed a finger at Jake's face. "Everyone who signed with me did so willingly. They were happy to get the money, and spreading rumors like that can get you into trouble."

"I'm only interested in the Burgess land." Jake's voice was cool. "Whatever else is about to bite you in the butt is your problem."

"Get out!" Josephson opened the door wider and shoved at Jake. "I only had a slight interest in the Burgess land when I spoke to them. It was on the fringes of the parcel that I was trying to put together. Now that I am no longer attempting to assemble that property package, I have no interest whatsoever."

"Something to consider." Jake didn't back away. "Having your daughter shredding evidence means that when you're caught, she'll be considered a coconspirator."

Ashley, who had clearly been eavesdropping, asked, "What's a coconspirator?"

Jake turned to answer her. "A person who gets the same punishment as the one who committed the crime."

As he left the real estate agency, he heard Ashley screech, "A new smartphone isn't worth it. I quit."

Driving to the dime store, Jake sighed. That

hadn't gone the way he expected. But at least he was fairly confident in crossing Josephson off his list. The guy might be doing something illegal, but it was doubtful that it had anything to do with the murder.

<u>CHAPTER 29</u>
Devereaux

I was seated at the soda fountain, responding to online basket requests on my laptop when I heard the little chime indicating that the rear door had been opened. I glanced up at the antique Bradley and Hubbard cast-iron looking glass hanging on the wall facing me, then smiled like a lovesick twelve-year-old when I saw Jake walking down the short hallway.

The gilt cherub on top of the mirror smirked at me as if the diminutive imp could read my mind. But if he were truly clairvoyant, his little round cheeks would be rosy red because, as always, Jake looked good enough to eat—or at least lick all over.

Glad that the last of the Knittie Gritties had left a few minutes ago and that the lunchtime rush was over, I saved the details of the orders to the proper file and closed the lid on the laptop. There were no customers in the store, and a quick glance at the vintage Ingraham schoolhouse clock assured me that the after-school crowd wouldn't arrive for another thirty minutes.

When Jake glanced my way, I motioned for him to join me. There were three stools at the counter, and I was sitting at the far end. He chose the middle one and lowered himself onto the red vinyl seat.

The tingling in the pit of my stomach when he took my hand reminded me of how much I loved this man. Then he gazed at me with those dark indigo eyes, making my heart stutter and my pulse kick up to record speed.

I could see the same response on his face too, and as much as I would have liked to drag him into the back room for a little afternoon delight, I throttled back the dizzying current running through me, cleared my throat, and asked a little breathlessly, "Did you find out anything from your two suspects?"

"Josephson is up to his neck in something shady." Jake's lips twitched, then he frowned. "But I'm convinced whatever the mess he's stumbled into, it isn't Burgess's murder."

"I'm not surprised. His business dealings have always been fishy." I got to my feet and went behind the counter. "Do you want something to eat or drink?"

"Coffee would be great." Jake leaned forward and grabbed an empty mug.

I poured the good stuff from my private pot into Jake's mug, then filled one for myself. "How about Blake Laudon? Did you find him?"

"Laudon answered the number I got from

Escobar's phone." Jake cradled his cup and inhaled the aroma of the piping-hot French roast. "He's agreed to talk to me at four in the B and B's parlor."

Grabbing a plate of baked goods—leftovers from the day's craft group meetings—I asked, "Is he staying at the bed-and-breakfast?"

"He will be as of four o'clock." Jake took a sip from his cup. "But he was in a hotel in Kansas City."

Sliding the dish and a stack of napkins next to Jake, I asked, "Did Blake resist coming in to talk?"

"Nope. He was downright eager." Jake's lips twitched. "He claims he was calling Escobar to apologize for overreacting and to renew their friendship. I told Laudon that I'd have Escobar present so he could make amends."

I sat down next to Jake and continued my questions. "But you won't have Quito there, right?"

"Correct." Jake nodded. "I want to see how Laudon reacts to the news of Burgess's death before I involve Escobar. If Laudon seems on the up-and-up, I'll inform our client and let him decide what he wants to do from there."

I nodded my understanding, then reached for a lemon-cranberry scone and said, "Tell me more about your encounter with Harry Josephson."

While we nibbled on pastries and drank our coffee, Jake described his encounter. We discussed the various criminal acts that the real estate guy might have committed, and before I knew it, high schoolers started pouring into the store and swarming up the stairs.

Happily, Taryn was leading the adolescent pack. My clerk and I didn't have time to exchange more than a quick greeting before he grabbed a cash drawer and a credit card reader and headed to the teen lounge.

During the continuing flood of young people, Jake put his hand on my arm and said, "I'll be in my office until I leave for the B and B. Will you have time to come with me to the Laudon interview?"

"I'll see if Dad can cover for me for an hour." I pulled out my cell from my back pocket and sent a quick text to him. "But now"—I scanned the customers crowding through the door—"I'd better get to work."

As usual, a few minutes after the kids arrived, my afternoon rush started. Shoppers were already three deep at the candy counter when I walked behind the display to help them.

The first woman in line placed her order for a pound of cookies-and-cream fudge, then, her eyes sparking with anticipation, said, "Did you hear about poor Aaron Burgess?"

As soon as she asked that question, I realized how odd it was that no one had mentioned Aaron's death earlier. Although, in thinking about it, the word probably hadn't spread as fast as most gossip did in Shadow Bend.

With Aaron living outside of town and his

murder occurring over the weekend, the rumor mill was probably a little slow to grind out the news. But now that it was out, everyone would be talking about it.

My hometown approached gossip like a spectator sport. And they fully expected a detailed play-by-play as well as front-row seats for the slo-mo reruns.

"I did hear about his passing," I said carefully, then tried to change the subject by handing her the small white box and asking, "Would you like anything else?" She shook her head and I gestured to my left. "Then you can pay at the register when you're finished with the rest of your shopping."

Before she could say anything more about the murder, the next person in line pushed forward. As I expected, most of my customers that afternoon wanted to discuss Aaron's death—both with me and with each other.

From what I managed to overhear, the county radio station had announced that a local farmer had died. The only detail they had was that the sheriff's department suspected that foul play was involved.

It was interesting that the reporter didn't announce anything about Aaron's cause of death. I was pretty darn sure if the information about his exposure to a toxic substance was known, it would have been the DJ's lead story, and it would have been what everyone was talking about. Evidently, the sheriff hadn't released the cause of death.

I worked steadily for the next hour, ringing up

sales and helping customers find their desired items, then as if by a magical tide, the crowd swept back out the door.

My father arrived, just as most of the shoppers made their exits. After we exchanged greetings, he walked over to the last few browsers, and I retreated behind the cash register, where I began to go over the messages on my cell phone. I had felt it vibrating while I was busy but hadn't had time to look at it.

The first text was from Beckham Janson, Birdie and Tony's home health aide. It was his daily check-in. He'd sent it at noon, but the cell gods had held on to it for several hours before allowing me to see it.

Luckily all the message said was that everything was going smoothly with our elderly Romeo and Juliet. I hadn't been worried, because Beck would have called if there were any real issues.

Still, I made a mental note that Jake and I should stop by after work. We hadn't been by to see Birdie and Tony since the move on Saturday, and I was determined not to neglect my grandmother just because I didn't live with her anymore.

The second message was from Jake, informing me that Laudon had called to say he was running late. The meeting had been pushed back to five.

Shoot! I had asked my father to come for an hour; now I'd have to see if he could stay until closing.

I was with Dad near the candy counter, asking him about remaining until the end of the day, when a breathtakingly beautiful woman stepped across the store's threshold. She had to be close to six feet tall. Although slim-hipped with broad shoulders, she wasn't at all boyish.

Everyone in the shop halted what they were doing and stared. She wore a sheer white long-sleeve off-the-shoulder top with a sleek black bra showing through the mesh. It stopped short of the waistband of her black leather pants, exposing two or so inches of her impossibly toned midriff.

She stood perfectly still in her high-heeled ankle boots, which I was pretty sure were Dior, then casually slung her Hermes handbag over her shoulder and strode the rest of the way inside.

Her long swath of brunette hair fell in a flawless curtain around her shoulders, and her straight white teeth were striking against her flawless olive skin. Her luminescent pale green eyes swept the store and zeroed in on my chest, which was a bit disconcerting until I realized she was reading the logo and not ogling my D cups.

It took me a few minutes to figure out why the striking woman looked familiar. Then it hit me. This imposing beauty was Rose Burgess.

Wasn't she just in Italy?

Wow! She got around more than a Baby Yoda meme on social media.

But what was she doing in my store?

CHAPTER 30
Devereaux

Rose Burgess didn't walk toward me as much as she glided in my direction. She was painstakingly stylish and moved as if she were strutting her stuff on a Paris runway. I had to admit that I was mesmerized observing her progress. It felt like I was watching a movie.

Without glancing either left or right, she crossed the space between the entrance and where I was standing. When she was a few steps away, my father nudged me with his elbow.

When I didn't react fast enough, he cleared his throat and whispered, "Shut your mouth before you swallow a bug."

Following his suggestion, I pasted a pleasant, and I hoped intelligent, expression on my lips, then I waited for the gorgeous woman to speak. I sure didn't know what to say.

I suppose I could have started with telling her I

was sorry about her husband's death. Or asked how Rome had been. Or even offered her a piece of fudge. But none of those things came to mind in time for me to say them.

Instead, after a moment of us staring at each other, she grabbed my hand and introduced herself as if she were a long-lost relative at a family reunion.

Eventually, she took a breath and said, "You are Devereaux Sinclair, right?" When I nodded, she continued, "My friend Quito speaks so highly of you, I couldn't wait to meet you."

"How sweet of him." I wasn't sure what he could have said about me, but, hey, as long as it was positive, I was okay with that. "He's said nice things about you too."

"He's such a sweetie." She dipped her head for a half a second, then looked up and said, "I'm here to see Jake Del Vecchio. I understand that he's helping Quito investigate my husband's death."

"That's correct." Finally, my brain kicked into gear and I added, "I'm so sorry for your loss." I gestured toward the ceiling and said, "Jake's office is on the second floor. My fiancé and I find it convenient to work in the same location." Chuckling, I continued, "We like to say that it cuts down on the commute."

Yes. I made a point to tell her that Jake was taken. I'm not proud of myself, but come on. She was a freaking supermodel. And I wasn't.

As she followed me, I added, "I suppose we really should put a sign in the window so people can find him. I'll show you the way."

We were halfway up the stairs when Jake met us coming down. I made the introductions and waited for him to turn around, but instead he just stared at me as if willing me to understand what he wasn't saying.

Usually, I was pretty good at keying into his nonverbal signals, but this time I wasn't able to interpret his expression. Widening my eyes and giving a tiny shrug, I let him know I was clueless.

An awkward minute later, Rose said, "Mr. Del Vecchio, I was hoping to talk to you about the investigation you're conducting on behalf of my friend Quito." She stepped around me, and as if we needed the clarification, she added, "Concerning Aaron's death."

"I'd be happy to fill you in, but I'm afraid I'm completely booked up today." Jake herded us down the staircase. "How about first thing tomorrow? We could meet here at nine and not have to rush."

"That would be fine." Rose bit her plump lower lip. "But would you have just a moment now?"

Jake seemed torn, then said, "If it's okay with Dev, maybe we could sit in the craft area until my next appointment." When I nodded, he led the way.

We all took a seat and Jake asked, "What can I do for you, Mrs. Burgess?"

I was delighted to see that he appeared unaffected by the woman's beauty, but not as thrilled when she leaned forward, put a hand on his, and said,

"Let's not be so formal. Please call me Rose."

"Of course." Jake moved his arm until it was out of her reach. "I'm Jake and you've already met my fiancée, Devereaux."

"I have." Rose seemed to understand Jake's subtle hint and gave us both a silk-edged smile.

Considering she'd made her living off of her good looks, I wasn't surprised that she would attempt to use them to get what she wanted. On the other hand, I gave her kudos for quickly recognizing that they didn't work on Jake. And that upsetting me wasn't a good idea either.

Jake waited a beat, and when it was clear Rose wasn't going to speak, he said, "I hate to rush you, but my next appointment is soon, so…"

"While I understand why Quito would like you to investigate Aaron's death"—Rose inhaled deeply— "and I fully support anything that keeps Quito out of jail, I think it would be more appropriate if I were your client since it's *my* husband who was murdered."

"Sorry, but that isn't possible." Jake shook his head. "I originally took this case because the local doctor had concerns, then when it turned out your husband's partner was a suspect, I terminated that agreement, and as a favor to my fiancée's best friend, I accepted a contract from Mr. Escobar." Jake shook his head again. "At this point, I'm unwilling to switch clients for a second time."

I was observing Rose carefully. A little line appeared between her perfectly arched brows. But she quickly caught herself and pasted an understanding expression on her face. I was pretty sure that she wasn't used to men refusing her requests.

"The thing is, I can afford your services more than Quito." Rose's glistening pink lips parted. "I don't want him to have to go into debt over this."

"Isn't that something you should discuss with him?" Jake asked.

"He probably isn't aware of my financial situation, and I'd prefer to keep it that way." Rose studied her smokey blue nail polish, then looked up and explained, "Aaron insisted that I keep the money that I had earned before we married in a separate account from our family funds, and we both signed a prenup saying that what was ours was ours."

Quito probably wasn't as financially comfortable as Rose and could use some help with Jake's fees, so I suggested, "Perhaps you could offer to split the cost with him."

"I suppose." Rose sighed, clearly not overjoyed with the idea. Gazing at Jake, she asked, "Would that make us co-clients?"

"No. As it stands…" Jake checked his watch.

When Jake didn't continue, Rose prompted, "You were saying…"

Jake stood. "Whoever signed my contract is my legal client." He held out his hand. "If you'd like to come in with Quito, we could try to sort this out tomorrow morning. Say around nine."

"But…" Rose stuttered as Jake walked away. She stared after him, then blew out an annoyed breath and turned to me. "Is he always that abrupt?"

I rose to my feet. "Only when he's busy." I escorted Rose to the exit. "Jake likes punctuality and hates keeping people waiting."

"I see." Rose waved. "Then I guess I'll see you tomorrow at nine sharp."

"I wouldn't miss it."

CHAPTER 31
Devereaux

After I escorted Rose Burgess to the front exit and saw her on her way, I checked on my father and Taryn. They both had their parts of the dime store under control, and I hurried into the storeroom to grab my purse, then rushed out the back door.

Fifteen minutes or so had elapsed when I finally climbed into Jake's pickup, and I figured that he was getting antsy at the delay. He confirmed my guess by throwing the truck into gear and driving out of the parking lot as soon as I fastened my seat belt.

Just as he turned onto the main drag, there was a flash of lightning and it started to rain. He flicked on the windshield wipers and headed toward the B and B.

Between thunder claps, Jake asked, "What did you think of Rose Burgess?"

"She's used to getting her own way and was quite surprised that you didn't react to her beauty."

"Not my type." Jake reached across and tapped my cheek. "As you well know."

I didn't. But I was happy to hear it.

"She really wants to be your client," I mused. "Then again, she probably has beaucoup bucks from her modeling career and wouldn't miss a few thousand for your fee." Something flickered across my brain that made me say, "I really need to take a look at those financial documents you photographed when you searched the Burgess house."

"I know you're busy, but the sooner you can do that the better." Jake pursed his lips. I could tell he was mulling over the encounter we'd just had with the vic's wife. "Either Rose is truly fond of Quito and wants to help him out…"

When he trailed off, I prodded, "Or?"

"Or," he continued, "she wants to control the investigation because she has some secrets she doesn't want revealed."

I thought about it and said, "Everyone has secrets, and I sure wasn't happy with my life being under the microscope when Noah's fiancée was murdered."

"Good point." Jake stroked his chin. "I don't think I have anything to hide, but you never really know until someone starts poking around in your past."

We were both silent until he pulled the pickup into the B and B's driveway. The huge Italianate-style house with the cute cupola in the center of the nearly flat roof was impressive. Its ornamental brackets and wraparound porch suggested a renaissance villa.

Jake and I exited the truck and hurried up the short sidewalk toward the front porch. The rain was pounding down, and I was happy that an engraved brass plaque mounted on the front door invited us to enter so that we could get out of the storm.

Stepping inside the large foyer, we used Jake's handkerchief to dry off, then headed to the reception desk nestled inside the curve of a beautiful wooden staircase. The owner, Veronica Ksiazak, a.k.a. Ronni, was busying typing on a laptop, but as soon as she noticed us, she closed the computer and slipped it out of sight.

"Dev, Jake." She came around the desk and smiled at us, her pretty blue-gray eyes sparkling with intelligence. "What a nice surprise."

"Hi, Ronni." I hugged her. "Now that Jake and I have finally moved in together, we need to have you and Coop over to the house for dinner."

I originally met Ronni at the Chamber of Commerce meetings. The town's women business owners had banded together to get our voices heard, and Ronni and I had found that we had a lot in common.

Although I was a native Shadow Bender, and Ronni had moved here a few years ago, her story was much like mine. She'd gotten tired of working in the city, bought the B and B and, with a thankful sigh, settled into the simpler life.

"That would be awesome." Ronni beamed. "When were you thinking?"

"How about Saturday?"

"I'll check with Coop, but I'm pretty sure we're free."

Before I could respond, Jake said, "We're here to see Blake Laudon. Has he arrived yet?"

"Yes, he's here. He's waiting in the parlor." Her brow creased. "He didn't mention that it was you two that he was expecting. I thought he said it was a guy named Quito something."

"Laudon must have misunderstood," Jake said as he ran a finger over the intricately carved mahogany of the newel post's finial cap. "What time did he arrive?"

"About ten minutes ago." Ronni led us to a small room off the foyer and then departed. She slid the doors closed behind her.

I'm not sure what I expected, but Blake was nothing like I had pictured him. He was just so average. Height, weight, brown eyes, and hair. For some reason, I guess I'd thought he'd be more imposing.

He was sitting in one of a pair of Louis XV armchairs, which were arranged in the middle of the room on top of an Oriental rug. And after we introduced ourselves, Jake and I took the matching cream damask settee.

We faced Blake over an ornate coffee table

comprised of six gold cherubs perched on top of a marble base holding up a glass top. Once we were settled, Blake asked, "Where's Quito?"

"He prefers we meet with you first, and then he'll decide whether he wants to see you," Jake lied smoothly.

With that, Blake abruptly burst into tears.

Jake and I sat there in silence until I leaned forward, grabbed a tissue from the box on the coffee table, and asked, "Mr. Laudon, are you all right?"

"I don't know." He took his hands away from his face and selected a Kleenex. He examined it as if searching for the perfect spot, then dabbed his eyes and blew his nose. "I'm just so disappointed that Quito isn't here." He pointed at Jake and choked out, "Mr. Del Vecchio promised that he'd arrange it."

"Which I will as soon as you answer a few questions for me." Jake's tone was sharp, and I immediately realized he was the bad cop in our partnership.

That left the good cop role for me, so I said, "One of the reasons that I'm here is that Quito is dating my best friend."

"He's in a relationship with a woman?" Blake's voice quavered and his blue eyes widened. "But I thought he and... I mean..." Blake trailed off, swallowed loudly, then asked, "What about Aaron?"

Before I could formulate my response, Jake jumped in. "Burgess is married to his high school sweetheart."

Is? I kept the question off my face, but why was Jake making it seem as if Aaron was alive? Was he hoping Blake would slip up and reveal that he already knew that his ex-friend was dead?

"Well…" Blake's pale forehead wrinkled. "The thing is I always thought Quito and Aaron were uh…you know…more than just friends."

"Not that I'm aware of." Jake crossed his arms. "Is that why you fought with Escobar and Burgess? You didn't approve of what you thought was their relationship?"

Interesting that Jake was pretending that he didn't know what had triggered the argument. Or did he think Quito had lied about it?

"No!" Blake shook his head vehemently. "That wasn't it at all."

He glanced at me. I nodded my encouragement. He smiled gratefully. I was beginning to like the good cop role.

"Actually, I was jealous." Blake picked at the cuticle of his thumb. "Not romantically." He checked my reaction, which he apparently found reassuring, then he went on, "But I always thought of us as the three musketeers, and when Aaron invited Quito to partner up with him to run the family farm, I felt excluded."

"Understandable." I stole a peek at Jake, and he seemed to want me to continue. "Were you familiar with rural life and working the land?"

"No." Blake sighed. "I was a city boy through and through." He smiled ruefully. "I'd never been out of the Chicago city limits before I joined the army."

"How about Quito?" I asked, since Jake was remaining silent.

"He grew up in the Central Valley of California." Blake moistened his lips. "His folks worked for an agribusiness near Fresno."

"Which made him a better choice." Jake leaned forward and demanded harshly, "Are you sure it wasn't your perception that they had a romantic relationship that caused you to blow up at them?"

"I'm positive." Blake wilted against the back of his chair. "It was me being a drunk."

"And now?" Jake snapped. "After all this time, why are you here?"

Jake had taken up the questioning, so it was my turn to observe. I had a good guess as to Blake's motivation but waited to see if I was right.

"I've been clean and sober for nearly a year," Blake explained.

Yep. As I suspected, he was working the AA steps. In my previous job, I had been around a lot of people in the program and could reel off the twelve steps faster than the Greek alphabet—which I'd had to be able to say three times to a match during my sorority days.

"I'm here to make amends to Quito and Aaron." Blake pursed his lips. "I wronged them both."

"Well," Jake paused then continued slowly. "I can certainly arrange for you to apologize to Escobar."

"Oh." Blake perked up.

"But not Burgess." Jake gazed at Blake without blinking.

"Because he won't see me?" Blake asked. "I sort of knew that. But maybe Quito can intervene for me."

"That's not the reason." Jake continued to stare at Blake. "You can't apologize to Burgess because he's dead."

"How…" Blake gasped. "I mean, he was a young man. What happened to him?"

"Someone murdered him." Jake leaned forward. "Was it you?"

"Oh, my gahhh…" Blake's eyelids fluttered and he clutched his chest. As he fainted, he slid to the floor with a thump.

Seconds later, Ronni ran into the parlor and screamed, "What did you do to my guest?"

CHAPTER 32
Devereaux

After we revived Blake, got him back in the chair, and ascertained that he hadn't hurt himself falling to the floor, we reassured Ronni that we hadn't done anything to her guest except tell him an old friend had died. It had taken a bit of an explanation, but she finally left us alone again.

Then Jake and I had to decide whether the whole fainting thing had been an act. While I was convinced that the man was really shocked at the news of Aaron's murder and had truly passed out, Jake was a lot more skeptical.

He eventually came around when Blake was able to produce an ironclad alibi for Saturday between noon and three. It turned out that in addition to being in Kansas City because of his desire to apologize to Quito and Aaron, Blake was there to see an endodontist. He explained that he had some kind of unusual issue with his teeth, and the KC guy was one of the few specialists that treated it.

He joked, "You know, a toothache is the only pain that drives you to extraction."

We politely chuckled, and Blake told us that he'd arrived for his appointment at twelve fifteen, been kept waiting for nearly forty-five minutes, and finally been called into the treatment room at one. His root canal had taken close to two hours.

A phone call to the dentist office had confirmed our suspect's story. As we said our goodbyes, Jake promised to contact Quito and ask him to get in touch with Blake.

Blake assured us that he'd be staying in Shadow Bend for at least a couple more days. He'd taken off of work for his dental treatment and wasn't due back until Monday, which meant he could give his old friend time to decide.

A few minutes later, we finally left the B and B and headed out of town to see Gran and Tony. During the short drive, we discussed the case but didn't come up with any new leads or conclusions.

It was well past six o'clock when Jake turned down the long driveway that led to Gran's house. It was located on the only ten acres she still owned of the extensive property my ancestors had settled in the eighteen-sixties.

Due to premature deaths, several generations of only children, and entire families packing up and moving away, Gran, my father, and I were the last Sinclairs in Shadow Bend. When Grandpa died fifteen years ago, Gran had begun selling off the land surrounding the old homestead to pay taxes and support herself. Piece by piece, I cringed as my heritage vanished, which was why I cherished what we had left.

I squinted through the rain as we passed the duck pond that we picnicked alongside every summer and the small apple orchard whose fruit we gathered in the fall for Gran's famous pies. There were a lot of good memories on this tiny oasis of land.

While it was no longer my home, it was still the place that had been my only refuge after my father went to prison and my mother walked out on me. I would always hold it dear to my heart.

We emerged from the tree-lined lane to a pool of artificial brightness created by the halogen light mounted on the garage. Like city streetlights, it turned on at dusk and off at sunrise, providing us with needed illumination on a moonless night.

Jake hopped out of the truck, and I followed suit, running to avoid the raindrops. By the time we got to the front door, Gran already had it open and beckoned us inside.

After hugging us, Gran led us to the kitchen and began filling the copper teakettle. Tony greeted us from his seat at the head of the table.

Even though he was in his eighties, Jake's great uncle was an imposing figure. Hard work had kept Tony lean and muscular. Like his grandnephew, he was tall and handsome, with the same intoxicatingly blue eyes. His hair might now be silver rather than black, but I could definitely see why Birdie was still in love with him.

Jolting me out of my thoughts, Beck poked his head in the kitchen and said, "I'll go watch my TV program while you all visit." Walking away, he added, "Let me know when you leave."

"That boy is so sweet." Gran got down the delicate china cups and saucers adorned with violets and wisps of curling ivy and put one in front of each of us.

I frowned at the cups. Gran only made tea when there was something serious that she wanted to discuss with me. Generally, she was more of a Jack Daniels type of gal.

While Tony and Jake chatted about the ranch and Gran continued to fuss with the tea leaves, I let my gaze wander around the kitchen. There was nothing fancy or new in the room, but everything reminded me of the home Gran had given me as an abandoned teenager.

After filling all our cups and setting a plate of cookies in the middle of table, Gran took a seat and demanded, "What's this I hear about Boone?"

"What did you hear?" I countered.

"That he has a boyfriend. I talked to his mom at the grocery store this morning, and she said that he told her and his dad on Monday that he was seeing someone and it was serious." Gran reached down and swooped up Banshee, her ancient Siamese.

I would have pulled back a bloody stump if I tried that trick with the cantankerous cat. Gran was the only one the feline allowed such liberties. He shot me a malevolent stare and made himself comfortable on her lap.

"Are you upset about that?" I asked, unsure about Gran's views on the matter of same-sex relationships.

"Why would I be?" She glared. "Just because I'm too old for a lifetime guarantee on a product to be worth much to me doesn't mean I'm narrow-minded."

"Of course not," I hastily assured her. "And you aren't that old."

Gran shook her head. "Sadly, when your wild oats turn into prunes and All-Bran, you really are."

"Nope." I shook my head. "You still have plenty of wild oats in you."

She wrinkled her brow but didn't argue, then said, "It's good to see Boone settling down with someone. Now we just have to get Poppy fixed up."

"That may be taken care of." I smiled, thinking about last night's call from Poppy. She'd squealed so loudly into the phone I'd thought for a minute that she'd burst my eardrum. "Noah finally came to his senses, dumped Meg, and asked her out."

As I mentioned Jake's ex, Tony slapped the table and chortled. "About time. Now maybe the Jezebel will get her butt out of Shadow Bend."

"She already has." Jake's grin matched his uncle's. "She's gone back to St. Louis."

"Good riddance to bad rubbish." Gran wiped her hands together as if dusting off crumbs. "Now. How about Boone's fellow? I hear he might have killed the guy he farms with."

"Where did you hear that?" Jake asked, frowning.

"My friend Freida called me. Her second cousin's granddaughter works for the sheriff's department transcribing all the recorded interviews." Gran straightened the crease on her bell-bottom jeans. "That girl is a terrible gossip."

Birdie's taste in clothing was eclectic at best. One day she'd wear a poodle skirt, and the next she'd have on a Jackie Kennedy suit—complete with matching pillbox hat and pumps.

"Someone should tell the sheriff that he has a leak in his department," Tony mused.

Jake raised his brows. "He might already know and use her for his own purposes."

"Anyway," I stepped into the conversation, "Jake and I are certain that Quito is innocent."

"Are you investigating the case?" Tony brightened and reached for a cookie.

"I am." Jake also picked up a snickerdoodle. "Unfortunately, all I've been able to do so far is eliminate other suspects."

"We'll find the killer." I patted Jake's hand and snatched the lone chocolate and vanilla pinwheel from the plate. "We still have Josh Camilo to interview. And if Aaron owed him money, he has a good motive to harm him."

"Josh Camilo? The guy who manages the motel out by the highway?" Gran asked.

Jake and I exchanged glances. We hadn't known where Camilo worked. That he was connected with the motel where Aaron and Meg had their trysts was very interesting. Suddenly he moved up several slots on our dwindling list of suspects. Maybe the cash that Aaron owed the man was blackmail money.

<u>CHAPTER 33</u>
Devereaux

We were driving home after finishing supper at Gran's. She and Tony had already eaten, but she insisted on heating up the leftovers for us. And since Gran's leftover fried chicken was a hundred times better than any restaurant food, we hadn't fought too hard when she started bringing platters to the table.

I was in a lovely digestive daze when, out of the blue, Jake asked, "Do think we'll ever find out why Birdie married your grandpa so soon after Tony went MIA in Korea?"

"I'm beginning to doubt it." Yawning, I lifted my head from where I had been resting it on the window and felt the last of my stupor slip away. "You saw how she reacted when you brought it up tonight."

Birdie had taken a sudden gulp of Jack Daniels, then drained the rest of the whiskey in her glass before saying that she didn't want to discuss it.

"I'm pretty sure Tony knows," Jake said, glancing at me as if to gauge my reaction.

"I agree." Rubbing the back of my neck, I added, "When he said that some things are best left in the past, he squeezed Gran's hand as if forgiving her."

"We should probably let the matter go, but I have to admit, my curiosity is killing me." Jake turned into the ranch's long gravel lane.

I yawned. "Maybe Tony will tell you if you get him alone and promise not to bring it up to Gran again."

Hopping out of the truck, we hurried inside. It was still raining and seemed as if it had no intention of stopping anytime soon.

Although it wasn't late, I was bushed. All I wanted was a hot bath, a glass of wine, and to get a good night's sleep. We had a lot to accomplish tomorrow, and I knew it would be exhausting.

* * *

The next morning, Jake and I drove into Shadow Bend together. He'd gotten up extra early to finish his ranching tasks, and when he came back inside for breakfast, he told me that he planned to devote the rest of the day to investigating Aaron's murder.

As were eating our omelets, Jake brought me up to speed on what he'd already learned that morning. While he was checking a fence line, he'd called Coop about the fire, but there was no news on that front.

Jake had also been in contact with the sheriff, who had confirmed that the fields close to the Burgess property hadn't shown any trace of the poison sprayed on Aaron. According to Kruse, the only residue they'd found was in the immediate vicinity of Aaron's tractor.

Now, we were on our way into town for the nine a.m. meeting with Rose. Later, we would track down Josh Camilo and interview him.

Luckily, I didn't have to work at the dime store until three. It had extended hours on Wednesdays, and my dad was covering the first shift, which left me with time to help Jake on the investigation.

In the past, before hiring Dad, I'd covered the entire day at the store myself, but now that my father was around, he'd taken some of the burden off of me. This allowed me to attend the meeting with Rose and go with Jake to talk to Josh Camilo at the motel afterwards.

However, I absolutely had to be back to the store by two thirty. Setting up for Blood, Sweat, and Shears, a philanthropic sewing group, took a lot of time and effort. Hauling out their tables, chairs, equipment, and supplies was a major operation, especially if I had to do it while also serving customers. My goal was to get most of it ready during the quiet period right before school let out, then finish up in the half-hour lull after five thirty.

The club's members would start to trickle in at six and wouldn't leave until late in the evening. They were supposed to wrap up by eight fifty, but at least one or two of the women always had to be pushed out the door so that I could finally close the store.

I wouldn't get home until close to ten tonight. At which time, I'd be both exhausted and ravenous. Not to mention a wee bit cranky. I hoped that Jake would already be asleep since he hadn't experienced my post Wednesday grouchiness yet.

With the store and the basket business thriving, I really needed to hire another clerk. The problem was finding someone reliable. Poppy always snapped up all the good candidates as soon as they became available, and since she paid a lot more than I could, plus tips, there wasn't a lot I could do to lure them to work for me instead.

My musings were interrupted when Jake parked the truck behind the store. There were already two other vehicles in the tiny lot. I recognized Boone's Mercedes, but the cute little Audi was unfamiliar.

Its bumper sticker made me chuckle. MONEY MAY NOT BE ABLE TO BUY HAPPINESS, BUT IT'S MORE COMFORTABLE TO CRY IN A LUXURY CAR THAN AN ECONOMY MODEL.

Still giggling, I followed Jake toward the store's rear door. As we approached, I saw Boone, Quito, and Rose waiting nearby.

Boone was dressed in a sharp suit. He was probably heading to his law office after this meeting. Quito wore jeans and a flannel shirt, ready to get into the fields once we were through. And once again, Rose had on an outfit worthy of lunching at a fancy New York restaurant.

She was absolutely stunning in a black sheath that highlighted a chunky gold bracelet, along with matching earrings and necklace. Her beige heels and calfskin brown purse were on the razor edge of fashion and I had to stop myself from drooling.

Although I loved them, designer outfits hadn't been in my budget since I bought the dime store. And with our marriage coming up, the only expensive item of clothing that I'd be purchasing this next year would be a wedding gown.

Greeting everyone, we all went inside. Jake, Boone, Quito, and Rose immediately proceeded to Jake's office. However, instead of following them, I made a detour to say hi to my father, who was already getting the store ready to open.

I told Dad to call me if he needed anything, then took the steps two at a time to catch up with the others. I met Jake carrying two folding chairs that he must have borrowed from the teen lounge.

It was a bit crowded with the extra seating arranged in front of the desk, but once we were settled, Jake said, "Rose, since you asked for this meeting, why don't you start?"

"Although Quito has turned down my offer to foot half your bill, he has graciously agreed to allow me be a part of your briefing."

"Okay." Jake took a folder from his top drawer and flipped it open. "Of the suspects we discussed, I have eliminated Harris Josephson and Blake Laudon. One was able to prove that he lacked a motive to kill the vic, and the other had an alibi."

"You spoke to Blake?" Quito asked, a line forming between his brows.

Jake nodded, then quickly summarized how he'd found the man and the results of our conversation with him, ending with, "Laudon is staying at the B and B. If you're willing to see him and hear his apology, give him a call."

"It might be good for you to get closure on that situation." Boone took Quito's hand. "You've mentioned how bad you felt about how things ended between you two."

"I'll think about it." Quito bit his lip, then looked at Jake. "The sheriff phoned me yesterday afternoon with more questions. He's really trying to pin this on me, isn't he?" When Jake shrugged, Quito begged, "Tell me that you have some other suspects."

Nodding, Jake turned to Rose and asked, "I understand your old boyfriend Brandon Tate was on some television program declaring his undying love for you. Has he contacted you since his divorce?"

I noted a tiny muscle tic at the corner of Rose's perfectly glossed mouth as she said, "He has not. I'm guessing he only said those things to get people talking about him again."

"Why would he want that?" I asked.

"Brandon lost quite a few lucrative endorsements deals during the initial scandal." Rose studied her nails. "And due to injuries, this past year, he's been off the field a lot. Which means he's been out of the public eye. My guess is he's hitting the talk shows to increase visibility and that his publicist told him to say I was his soul mate in order to make him look more sympathetic."

Jake didn't seem altogether convinced, but he shrugged and said, "Then I guess my next move is to talk to Josh Camilo." He looked at Rose. "Were you aware that he and your husband had a fight in Gossip Central?"

"No." Rose's eyes widened. "That really surprises me. Aaron wasn't a violent man. Do you know what the altercation was about?"

We didn't. At least no details. Mostly because when I questioned Poppy as to whether she had a recording of that incident, she told me that Josh and Aaron where in a dead area. There were just some spots that she was unable to plant a listening device, and she wasn't happy about it.

Tenting his fingers, Jake said, "From what I was told, Camilo accused your husband of owing him money."

"That's ridiculous." Rose's voice rose. "Although we kept our accounts separate, Aaron knew that I'd gladly give him whatever funds he needed." She shook her head. "What reason could he have had to borrow from that man?"

Jake closed the file, indicating the meeting was over. "That's what I intend to find out when I talk to Camilo."

"You're wasting your time." Rose folded her arms across her chest. "Whoever claimed Aaron and this Josh person were fighting was either mistaken or a liar. You'd do better to point your investigation in another direction."

Jake and I glanced at each other and he raised a brow. I gave a slight nod. Why was Rose reacting so weirdly to the news we were going to talk to Josh Camilo?

While everyone got to their feet, I thought about everything Rose had said. It was definitely time for me to look at the financial records Jake had obtained when he searched the Burgess home. I had some forensic accounting in my future.

<u>CHAPTER 34</u>
Jake

Jake glanced at his watch as he pulled out of the dime store's parking lot. It was ten thirty, which gave Devereaux four hours to examine the Burgess financial records before her shift started downstairs.

Although Jake had long since printed out the pictures he'd taken after searching the vic's house, Devereaux hadn't had time for any in-depth scrutiny. Sure, she'd taken a casual glance through the documents, but she had seen nothing suspicious. As he'd suspected, there was nothing obviously wrong with the Burgesses' fiscal situation.

The farm appeared to be in the black, the household bills were all paid on time, and their mutual savings and checking statements appeared relatively healthy. Jake hadn't seen any evidence of Rose's separate investment account, and once he realized that, it seemed odd that those records weren't with the others.

Evidently, Devereaux felt the same way, because

when Rose had mentioned her and her husband's fiscal arrangement, Jake had noticed Devereaux's subtle stiffening. Then once everyone had left the office, she asked if he'd mind talking to Camilo alone while she performed what she called a forensic deep dive on the Burgess documents.

From working as a marshal, Jake vaguely understood that term to mean a compilation of economic evidence, which she would then feed into a computer program that she had designed for her use when she worked as a financial consultant.

As Jake headed toward the highway, he thought about the situation. He would have liked to have had Devereaux along as an extra set of ears. However, considering the man managed a no-tell motel, Camilo might turn out to be more comfortable talking to Jake alone.

Or maybe it was Jake that would be more comfortable. He hated exposing Devereaux to a place, or person, that sleazy. Of course, he'd never admit that to his fiancée, who would doubtlessly tell him that she didn't need him to protect her delicate sensibilities because she wasn't a fragile flower who would swoon at the slightest bit of impropriety.

He pulled his pickup into the motel's lot a few minutes later, still chuckling about the image of his fiancée as a Victorian maiden. Which made his mind leap to waking up that morning with Devereaux in his arms.

Parking his truck, Jake took a moment to recall the feeling of her soft curves pressed against him and the smell of her fiery yet sweet perfume. It had been agony getting out of the warm bed to go do his chores.

However, the adorable look on her pretty face as she slept had prodded him out the door. He intended to make the Del Vecchio ranch one of the most successful spreads in Missouri. He was determined to ensure that Devereaux and their children would always have whatever they needed. He also meant for Tony's and Birdie's lives to be as comfortable as he could make them.

Jake still hadn't quite gotten used to being primarily a rancher or working on the private side of law enforcement, instead of as a part of the marshal service. But after he'd been injured, quitting and settling down in Shadow Bend had been the right decision. Tony had needed help with the cattle operation, and Devereaux had needed him to be around full-time.

It turned out that there was more to life than the adrenaline rush of chasing bad guys. And Jake suddenly realized that he was happier now than he'd ever been.

Although Jake had wanted to be a US Marshal since his sixth-grade social studies teacher had shown the class a documentary about the service, looking back, his retirement had seemed preordained.

Between his own injury and his uncle's age, fate had been nudging him into the right decision. And meeting Devereaux had cinched the deal.

With one last smile at the thought of his new life, Jake reluctantly set aside his daydreams of the feisty cinnamon-haired woman he loved so much it hurt and concentrated on the case. There was something about Camilo and the vic's fight that itched just below the surface of Jake's subconscious. It had to be about Burgess's infidelity. Could Camilo have been blackmailing Burgess?

Exiting the cab, Jake marched into the tiny office. He rang the bell for service, but no one responded. He was about to tap it again when he heard a faint rustling from the room behind the motel's check-in counter.

Resting his hand on his weapon, Jake was thankful that Missouri allowed concealed carry. He'd obtained a permit at the same time he'd applied for his PI license and realized that he should have Devereaux get her permit too. Not only would she be able to defend herself better, she'd look smoking hot with a garter holster strapped to her thigh.

Forcing himself to concentrate on the present situation, Jake yelled, "Anybody here?"

Had someone beat him here and shut up Camilo before he could spill the beans? Jake called out again, and when there was no answer, he debated what to do. Should he call the police?

Before he could decide, a spotted hound with droopy ears moseyed around the counter. It was followed by a thirtyish man carrying a plastic bag.

The dog woofed a greeting at Jake, then padded slowly to a large plaid doggy bed in the corner of the room. He gave a final woof, then flopped down and closed his eyes.

Jake removed his hand from his weapon and addressed the guy staring at him. "Are you Josh Camilo?"

"Yeah." The guy seemed surprised to be addressed by name and added, "Can I help you?"

"I understand that you're the manager here?"

"Yeah," the guy grunted, then jerked his chin at the dog. "Sorry I wasn't here, but it seems the only time the world beats a path to my door is when the old girl needs to take a piss."

"Jake Del Vecchio." Jake shook hands. "I'm a private investigator."

"What can I do you for?" Camilo's muddy-brown eyes held a spark of interest.

"I understand you had an altercation with Aaron Burgess over at Gossip Central," Jake said. "Can you tell me what it was about?"

Camilo took a step backwards. "I heard he got himself killed. You think it was me that done it? 'Cause I got an alibi. I was visiting my sister in Chicago last weekend. I left Friday night and didn't get back until Sunday around noon."

"Good to know." Jake nodded reassuringly. "Then you won't mind telling me about your issue with Burgess."

"Well…" Camilo licked his lips. "The guy was into me nearly a hundred bucks."

"How did he end up owing you money?" Jake asked. "Gambling? Drugs?"

"Hell no!" Camilo yelled. "I don't make book and I don't sell dope."

"But you do look the other way when pros rent a room for an hour." Jake wanted to make sure the guy was aware that the motel's reputation wasn't lost on him.

"Hey." Camilo shrugged. "I see it like this. They ain't two-bit whores as much as they're low-cost providers."

"Right." Jake rolled his eyes, then asked, "Did Burgess owe you money for that type of service?"

"I ain't no pimp and I ain't no stool pigeon." Camilo's tone was one of outrage, but then he wrinkled his brow and said, "On the other hand, I guess it don't matter now. He owed me for the room, not the piece of tail. He and this scary chick were regular customers, and he couldn't use his credit card 'cause he was married and didn't want to upset his wife."

"How thoughtful." Jake couldn't keep the scorn from his voice.

"Well, ya know." Camilo grinned. "A man needs a mistress just to break up the monogamy."

Jake rolled his eyes again. This guy thought he was a lot funnier than he actually was.

Attempting to get the conversation back on track, Jake said, "Then Burgess paid you in cash."

"Mostly." Camilo shrugged. "But the last few times, he was short and asked if he could float a loan until he sold some crops."

"The woman he was with couldn't use her card?" Jake asked.

Camilo snorted. "No way, no how. She was real mad that he even asked."

"Interesting." Jake thought Devereaux might be right in suspecting Meg. "Well, thanks for the info."

Jake turned to leave, but Camilo said, "I sure hope you're the last one coming out here to ask about the guy. I would've never lent him the money if I knew he'd go and get himself killed."

"Was the sheriff or his deputy here?" Jake wondered how Kruse had found out about the debt.

"I don't think this gal was no cop." Camilo smirked. "She was way too hot for that." He shrugged. "Besides, she was here a month or more ago. Way before Aaron was offed."

"What did the woman look like?" Jake asked.

"Tall with a pretty nice rack, even though it was a little small for my taste." Camilo scratched his crotch. "Long dark hair and real unusual green eyes."

"She didn't give you her name?" Jake was pretty sure the guy had just described Rose Burgess.

"Nah." Camilo folded his arms. "But she paid me a couple of hundred bucks to tell her all about Aaron and his floozy."

"Did she say how she came to ask you about them?" Jake asked.

"She found some text on his phone," Camilo tittered. "She didn't say, but if I had to guess, it was Aaron's wife."

"You're probably right."

"Yep." Camilo shook his head. "But why someone would want to screw that scary chick if he had that stunner at home is beyond me."

"Me too."

Jake knew that Meg was good at manipulation. She'd certainly worked him. But he hadn't been involved with anyone else at the time, let alone been married to a supermodel.

After thanking Camilo for his help, Jake headed back to his truck. Once he was settled behind the wheel, he sat in the cab for a few minutes digesting what he'd learned. Rose would be the perfect suspect for Burgess's murder, if only she didn't have such a good alibi. How could she be at the Kansas City airport and spraying poison on her husband at the same time?

CHAPTER 35
Devereaux

I sat back and rubbed my eyes. They were burning from going back and forth between the pages of data and the computer screen.

After Jake left, I had poured myself a cup of coffee, selected a blueberry, lemon, and thyme muffin from the daily bakery delivery, grabbed my laptop, and headed upstairs to work in Jake's office.

I could have set up in the dime store's back room, but it was much more comfortable, not to mention quiet, on the second floor. Until the teen lounge opened, I was the only living soul on this level of the building.

Maybe it was too quiet and that's why I wasn't finding anything significant. At first glance, it hadn't been obvious that the couple had their own credit cards, their own bank accounts, and their own investments because Rose managed it all. She paid the bills, put money in their accounts, and dealt with their portfolios, but everything financial was kept separate.

It was almost as if they had been roommates instead of husband and wife.

The farm accounts were another matter. They were in both Aaron's and Quito's names, with Rose acting as bookkeeper. From what I could tell, when Aaron had invited Quito to be his partner, Quito had put up fifty percent of the value of the land as his buy-in and was an equal partner with Aaron.

I had a yellow pad, where I listed any questions that arose from my examination. Number one was how had Quito come up with the money he'd used to pay Aaron?

As I continued to add the information into the forensic computer program that I was using, my gaze kept sliding to the time at the lower right corner of the screen. It was nearly two, and I would have to stop soon to start setting up for the sewing club.

I had just finished putting in the last of the items Rose had purchased using her American Express during the past year when I heard the sound of cowboy boots climbing the stairs. I smiled in anticipation of seeing my fiancé's handsome face and began to gather up the documents that I had spread across his desktop.

A few seconds later, Jake strolled through the door and said, "How're you doing, sugar?"

"I managed to get all the info into the program." I tapped a pile of pages into alignment and put them into the proper folder.

Jake hung up his hat and coat, then walked over and peered into the laptop's monitor. "Did you find anything?"

"Nothing leaped out at me." I clicked so that he could see the couple's credit card statements. "Aaron mostly used his Visa at the gas station and Gossip Central, but Rose's AmEx is a different story."

Jake ran his finger down the long line of purchases, and as he reached one that was dated a few weeks ago, I yelled, "Stop."

There was a charge for two thousand forty-nine dollars from a company called Definitive UAV. Most of Rose's expensive purchases were identifiable as being from clothing and department stores. For some reason, I hadn't noticed this one when I'd entered the information.

"What do you see?" Jake squinted and leaned closer to the screen.

"I just don't recognize that company." I highlighted the line, copied the name, and brought up Google. "I want to see what they sell."

I pasted Definitive UAV into the search engine. A few seconds and a couple of clicks later, I was at the Definitive Unmanned Aerial Vehicles website.

Frowning, I looked at Jake and asked, "Why would Rose want to buy a drone?"

Jake sucked in an audible breath of air and said, "So she could use it to spray poison on her husband while creating an ironclad alibi."

"But why would she want to kill him?" I asked.

"Everything we've found out about him points to him being a pretty nice guy."

Jake cocked an eyebrow. "Except for his affair with Meg, right?"

"Rose didn't know about that." I frowned as it dawned on me that Jake had information that he hadn't shared with me yet. "Or did she?"

"She sure as shooting did." Jake perched on the desk facing me.

Narrowing my eyes, I pointed at him and demanded, "Tell me everything."

Jake went over his encounter with Josh Camilo, then, in his US Marshal voice, said, "To summarize, about a month ago, Rose saw a text from Meg about meeting at the motel. She then bribed Camilo into spilling the beans and found out her husband was sleeping with another woman."

"Which is why she killed him." I tapped my chin. "If that's true, Meg was smart to get out of town before Rose figured out she was Aaron's lover."

"I wondered why the last time Meg contacted me, it was from a different cell phone." Jake smiled wickedly. "I'm guessing that after Rose got rid of her husband, she sent a threat to the number connected to the text that Aaron had received about meeting him at the motel."

Aware that none of the info Jake had found at the Burgess house could be used in court, I asked, "Could that message be used as evidence?"

"Possibly." Jake shrugged. "But knowing Meg, that text has long since been deleted."

"Maybe the sheriff can get the records from the cell phone company."

"He'd need probable cause, and Meg would never admit that such a message ever existed." Jake squeezed my shoulder. "We'll have to get Rose to confess."

"Easy-peasy." I snapped my fingers. "One other problem with your theory."

"Oh?"

I pointed to the paragraph with the details for the UAV. "According to this website, the maximum distance that a civilian drone can fly is a little over six miles. If Rose was at the airport, she was ten times that far away."

"Except…" Jake's navy-blue eyes sparkled. "I remember one case that I worked when I was a marshal, where the drug lord had synced a drone to his smartphone and was able to keep an eye on his mules even though he was hundreds of miles away. He had the drone stashed near the border and could see exactly when the coyote got them across."

"So, before Rose left for Kansas City on Saturday, she could have set up her drone near the field where her husband would be working." I could barely contain my excitement at finally figuring out how Aaron had been sprayed.

"Right." Jake seemed to share my satisfaction. "Then once she was checked in at the airport and had her alibi established, she used her smartphone or her laptop to fly the drone and deliver its payload."

"Do you think she's retrieved the drone since then?" I counted on my fingers. "It's been four days."

"She might have." Jake tapped his chin. "That could be why Escobar's trailer was burned down. The field where she'd have staged the drone is pretty close to his place, and if she tried to go pick it up while he was living there, he might have seen her."

"But she could just fly it back to her house." I played the devil's advocate.

"It was probably out of power." Jake tapped the computer screen, and he read aloud, "'Typical drones usually last for twenty to thirty minutes in the air before their battery is drained. Flight time is lessened depending on weight of payloads.' Adding the spraying device and the toxic liquid would probably cut that time in half."

"Let's see." I stared at the ceiling. "Rose was out of the country on Saturday and most of Sunday. Then when she got back, it was dark and she was busy setting fire to Quito's trailer."

Jake continued my timeline. "Rose had to return to work early Monday morning, and from what she said yesterday afternoon, she'd just gotten into town when she came to try to hire me—which, by the way, I now understand why she wanted to be my client. It was so she could control the investigation."

"That means Rose had yesterday evening and

today to retrieve the UAV."

"True," Jake agreed. "However, if she ran it out of power, she wouldn't know exactly where the drone had landed, and we had those storms blow through here yesterday just after she left the store."

"Although she might have gone searching for the UAV before she met with us this morning, she certainly wasn't dressed like she'd been tromping through the fields." I narrowed my eyes, thinking. "And weren't she and Quito going over to the funeral home after our meeting to make arrangements?"

"Right." Jake smiled wolfishly. "They had an eleven o'clock appointment. That had to take a couple of hours." He glanced at his watch. "At the most, she's had an hour to search. And that's only if she was able to shake Quito afterwards."

"Didn't he say he planned on getting back into the fields this afternoon?" I asked.

"Yep." Jake nodded. "He planned to finish the field Aaron had been working, then put that antique tractor in the shed. Which would have put him in her way if she wanted to search for the drone."

I looked at my watch. Depending on how much time the funeral arrangements took, there was a good chance that Quito had probably finished planting that field within the last hour or so.

"We have to go look for that drone right now." I leaped to my feet. "If we're lucky, either we get to it before Rose or we find her looking for it."

Jake grabbed his hat and jacket, then held the

office door open for me. "Let's go."

CHAPTER 36
Devereaux

By the time this case was finally wrapped up, I would owe Dad big-time. Maybe I'd pay for an overnight package in a nice hotel in Kansas City for him and his girlfriend, Catherine.

My father had agreed to continue working until I got back, and I'd made him promise to have Taryn help him set up for the Blood, Sweat, and Shears before they opened up the teen lounge. The kids could pitch in and move some furniture themselves if they didn't want to wait for their space to become available.

Now, Jake and I were on our way to the Burgess fields to see if we could beat Rose to the drone. Or at least discover her retrieving it.

As we drove, I said, "Maybe we should call your friend the sheriff and let him in on what we've discovered, as well as our current plans."

"That's probably a good idea." Jake pulled his cell from his shirt pocket and handed it to me. "Dial for me, darlin', then put it on speaker."

Thankfully, the sheriff had given Jake his private number, and he picked up on the first ring. While Jake went over our theory and how we'd reached it, I thought about how enraged Rose must have been to go to such elaborate lengths to kill her husband. Most women would have just divorced the guy.

Tuning back in, I heard the sheriff say, "All my on-duty deputies are tied up in a multicar crash over on the other side of the county, and I'm stuck in traffic coming back from Kansas City. But I'll try to get someone to that field as soon as I can."

"Do you want us to wait?" Jake asked, scowling. "She might get rid of the evidence, and without it, there's no case."

"No." Sheriff Kruse paused. "You go ahead, just make sure you record everything. Especially if you catch Rose in the act."

When I'd been studying for my private investigator's license, I had learned that Missouri was a one-party consent state. As long as one of the participants consented, recording an interaction was perfectly legal.

In situations like this one, that was such a blessing. I pitied my friends Skye and Dani, who lived in Illinois, where both parties had to agree to be recorded. It was almost as if that state wanted criminals to go free.

With assurances he or a deputy would be there as soon as possible, the sheriff ended the call.

When Jake remained silent, I asked, "Any idea where we should start our search?"

I was taken aback when he just chuckled and pointed. But then I took a look in the direction he was indicating and snickered. A tiny figure was trudging right toward us.

Jake immediately pulled over and took a pair of binoculars from the glove box. After he looked through them, he handed them to me. The person walking through the field was Rose, and she appeared to be carrying a giant black spiderlike object in her arms. I could now see why Aaron had thought he'd been attacked by a pterodactyl.

As we watched, she noticed the pickup and froze. An instant later, she whipped her head around, then, obviously realizing there wasn't any place to hide, she kept walking.

From where we were sitting, we could see Rose's house across the road to the right. And we had passed Quito's trailer a couple miles behind us.

"Now what?" I asked.

"We make her believe that we have more evidence than we do and are willing to take a bribe to keep our mouths shut." Jake opened the truck door and came around to help me out. Once I was next to him, he said, "Get ready to record our conversation."

"Okay." I reached into my purse, took out my cell, unlocked it, and tapped the voice memo icon. Putting it into the pocket of my jacket, I rested my finger on the red circle and whispered, "Go ahead."

Jake stated the date and location, then said, "I, Jake Del Vecchio, hereby give my permission to Devereaux Sinclair to record my conversation with Rose Burgess."

A few seconds later, when Rose stepped out of the field and onto the shoulder of the road, Jake said, "Mrs. Burgess, fancy meeting you here."

Her expression unruffled, she twitched her shoulders. "Why is that? I own this land, or I will once Aaron's estate is settled."

"That you do." Jake nodded affably. "I see you found your drone."

Rose lifted her chin. "This isn't mine. I was looking out my living room window, and I saw it touch down, so I went to see what had landed on my property."

Jake reached into his shirt pocket, took out his notebook, and tapped it on his palm. "It's all here. You might as well confess."

"What in the world are you talking about?" Rose fluttered her lashes. "I have nothing to confess."

"How about we start with you killing your husband?" Jake crossed his arms.

"You're aware that I have an alibi." Rose shook her head. "I know you can't be crazy enough to think I could magically transport myself from the airport to here within the time constraints of the murder."

"Your alibi flew out the window, pun intended, the minute we realized you used a drone to deliver the malathion." I decided to enter the conversation.

"How in the world would I do that?" Rose raised a brow. "These toys can't fly all the way from Kansas City to here."

"They can if you stage them nearby and use your smartphone or tablet to control them." Jake's tone was blunt.

Rose's voice was breathy. "Why would I want to kill Aaron? I loved him."

"That may or may not have been true at one time." Jake's expression was impassive. "But the minute you found out he was cheating on you at the local no-tell motel, that love turned to hate."

"You're confusing me," Rose frowned. "What do you mean? Aaron wasn't having an affair."

I stared at her and said, "Josh Camilo ratted you out."

Jake turned to another page in his notebook. "About a month ago, you found a text on your husband's phone from a woman arranging a rendezvous. You then proceeded to investigate and confirmed that he and this woman had been regular customers at the motel. At which time, you began plotting his death."

Rose waved off Jake's words. "That's ridiculous. I'd have no idea how to fly a drone or use it to spray poison at my husband."

"You're a smart, successful woman." I tipped my head at Rose. "I bet you can figure out almost anything or persuade one of your pilot friends to teach it to you." Then, taking a gamble because I hadn't looked up her high school record, I said, "After all, you graduated in the top of your class."

"There's wasn't much competition." Rose tipped her head, attempting to use her charm on Jake. "I'm sure you understand that the plot you've outlined is beyond my capabilities."

"Once we've finished our little conversation here, I'll be contacting Sheriff Kruse, who will get a warrant to look at your credit card accounts, where I'm sure he'll find a record of your purchase for that drone in your arms, as well as the malathion," Jake warned. "He'll also interview every single pilot you ever worked with."

I glanced at Jake and he gave a tiny nod, so I said, "The sheriff will also get a warrant for your phone and Aaron's phone. He'll find the app that controls the drone on yours, and the text messages from the other woman on your husband's."

"I..." Rose finally put the drone down and rubbed her arms as if she were suddenly cold. "This isn't how it looks."

"What it looks like is that you killed your husband and burned down Escobar's trailer so he wouldn't see you searching the fields for the drone," I pounced.

"Uh." Rose seemed to belatedly realize she was being backed into a corner. She then raised her chin and said, "How much would it take for you not to make that phone call to the sheriff?"

"I doubt you can afford our price." I pasted an avaricious smile on my face.

"How does half a million sound?" Contempt tainted Rose's gorgeous green eyes, and arrogance lurked at the corners of her perfect cupid's bow lips.

"Just to be clear," Jake drawled, "you're willing to pay us a half a million dollars to forget what we've found out, and for us to neglect to inform the sheriff that you killed your husband."

"Yes." Relief oozed out of that one word. "I can get you a cashier's check by tomorrow morning."

"First tell me why you killed him. I don't understand." Jake frowned. "Why you didn't just divorce Burgess? You said that you kept your money separate, so it can't be a financial motive."

"Because I was sick and tired of men using me." Sweat glistened on Rose's forehead. "First it was all those photographers that I had to sleep with to get decent pictures for my portfolio. Then it was the ad reps who insisted on a piece of me. And when I finally thought I found someone who loved me, Brandon turned out to be married and threw me under the bus."

"But Aaron was your high school sweetheart, and you thought you could trust him." I nodded my understanding. "You figured that you'd come back to your small town, where things were simpler and people were more honest."

"That's right." Rose wrinkled her nose. "Not like

those sleazebags and liars that live in New York and LA."

It was a little rude, but I had to ask. "What I don't understand is why Aaron, who otherwise seems like a decent guy, would want to cheat on someone who looks like you."

"I don't know either. Maybe it was my sexual limitations. His taste was a little freakier than I realized and I couldn't handle it. Or maybe I shouldn't have taken the flight attendant job and been away from home so much." Rose's expression held a wealth of sadness. "But I was bored and Aaron said he didn't mind." Her shoulders slumped. "I guess he did though, huh?"

We were all silent for a minute, then I said, "So you killed your husband because he was like all the other men who let you down or used you?"

"Yes." Rose scowled. "He had to be punished, and since I'd signed the prenup, I couldn't take his farm, so I took his life."

Jake reached down and lifted the drone into his arms. "We'll just keep this for a little insurance."

"I want that back when I give you the check tomorrow," Rose snapped.

"Sadly, I don't think we'll be picking up that check after all."

"Why not?" Rose sputtered.

"Hear that?" Jake jerked his thumb over his shoulder, and we all looked to where he was pointing.

The sheriff's car was racing our way with lights and sirens flashing.

"What did you do?" Rose slapped Jake across his face.

"The right thing." A red handprint stood out on Jake's cheek.

A few seconds later, the cruiser pulled to a stop. Sheriff Kruse stepped out of the vehicle with his gun drawn.

At Jake's nod, he approached Rose. He recited the Miranda warning as he handcuffed her. A single tear rolled down her cheek as he put her in the back of the car.

I was impressed that Kruse had trusted Jake enough to make the arrest without asking any questions first.

A few seconds later, the sheriff walked back to where we were standing and asked, "You do have her recorded confession, right?"

"We do." Jake glanced at me. "We'll send it to you, along with a summary of the evidence that we've gathered, as soon as we get back to town."

The sheriff stuck out his hand. "Thanks for the help. I owe you one."

Watching the cruiser pull away, I said, "That was nice of him."

"It was." Jake put his arm around me and squeezed.

"Not to mention it might come in handy to have a marker with the county sheriff."

I leaned into his embrace. "Yep. Especially since you never know what our next adventure might entail."

EPILOGUE

The past couple of weeks had been a whirlwind of action. Jake and I had given our statements to the sheriff and been interviewed by the county prosecutor. We'd been called in again and again as the case the progressed, and it was a relief when Rose's attorney finally brokered a plea agreement.

Once the bizarre story got out about the manner in which Rose had killed her husband, the media had descended on Shadow Bend like leprechauns on a field of four-leaf clovers.

Between the James Bond-like murder weapon and Rose's previous fame, our little town was flooded with journalists representing every form of news outlet from the print tabloids to the gossip television programs to the celebrity bloggers. And they all wanted to talk to Jake and me.

At first, I attempted to steer clear of everyone by putting my father in charge of the dime store, holing up at home, and refusing to answer either the door or the phone. Jake pretty much followed my example, sticking to the ranch and screening his calls.

After my own brush with the law a few years ago, I had vowed to avoid the spotlight with the same zeal that I did the scale in the bathroom. However, after days of having his ranch hands escort members of the Fourth Estate off his property, Jake had persuaded me that our best course of action was to give a press conference.

His argument was that if we answered everyone's questions, the journalists would quit trying to scoop each other. Once we'd told our stories, there wouldn't be any reason left for them to try to be the first one to talk to us.

Not that I'd ever admit it to him, but, as usual, he was right. As soon as we cooperated with the paparazzi, they left us, and Shadow Bend, alone.

Now, as I sat in Gossip Central, I couldn't help but smile. It was Saturday evening, and things had finally returned to normal. Poppy and Noah, Boone and Quito, and Jake and I were celebrating the official resolution of Aaron's murder.

We were in our new favorite alcove, the one nicknamed the Lodge. It had a romantic fireplace and a trio of comfy sofas. Each of the three couples had claimed one of the couches and were cuddled together on it. The sofas formed a U shape around a large occasional table that held snacks, a pitcher of margaritas, and a bucket of beers.

Poppy refilled her glass and asked, "What's

happening with your trailer, Quito?"

"As soon as Rose confessed to setting the fire, the insurance company cut me a check," he answered.

"Tell them the rest," Boone urged, a huge smile on his face.

I thought for a minute they were announcing that they were moving in together, but instead Quito said, "Aaron named me as his secondary beneficiary in his will. And because of the slayer rule, a person can't inherit property from a person they murder, so I'm now the sole owner of the farm, which includes the house."

"Wow." I blinked, then added, "That's great."

Everyone nodded, then Noah asked, "Any idea what will happen to Rose?"

Jake rolled his eyes. "Her attorney managed to get the prosecutor to take first-degree murder, which could result in the death penalty, off the table. In exchange, she pled guilty to voluntary manslaughter, claiming that although she thought the poison would make Aaron sick, she never dreamed it would kill him."

"So, what? Fifteen years?" Boone shook his head. "And probably up for parole in five?"

"That's so unfair!" Poppy shrieked.

"You're right," I agreed. "Which is why I'm determined to testify at every one of her parole hearings."

Apparently, the alcohol was starting to affect me, because I hadn't thought about doing that until I blurted it out. Still, it was a good idea.

"I will too," Quito vowed.

With that, our conversation turned to more lighthearted matters, and after a couple more rounds of margaritas, I looked at Noah and teased, "So how many women threatened Poppy with bodily harm once the gossips realized you two were dating?"

"Seriously?" Noah's tone was scornful, then he put his arms around Poppy and gave her a long kiss. "Anyway, if that were true, there would be just as many men wanting to get me out of the picture."

Boone shook his finger. "Remember, we've all agreed to no public displays of affection."

"Yes, sir." Poppy crossed her heart. "We'll behave if you will."

Giggling, we continued to eat and drink until I heard my phone chirp. I excused myself and headed to the ladies' room. Once I was in the bathroom stall, I checked the message. There was no identification and it just said: I'LL BE IN SHADOW BEND SOON AND NEED YOUR HELP.

Crossing my fingers that the text had been sent to a wrong number, I deleted it and returned to the party. If it was meant for me, I'd think about it when whoever sent it showed up at my door, and not a minute before.

THE END

Thank you for reading Fly Me to the Tomb. I'm thrilled you chose to spend your time with my characters and I hope you enjoyed their story.

Reviews help other readers find the books they want to read. So before you go, please leave a review, tweet, share or recommend it to your friends.

Join me on Facebook [http://www.facebook.com/DeniseSwansonAuthor] or visit my website [http://www.DeniseSwanson.com] or follow me on Twitter [DeniseSwansonAu].

Subscribe to the Denise Swanson e-newsletter for quarterly or semi-annual updates about her books and events, plus occasional recipes and other news!

Write to Denise at **ScumbleRiver@aol.com** with **Subscribe** in the Subject line and your own **E-Mail Address, First Name** and **Last Name** in the Body:

Send To:	ScumbleRiver@aol.com
Subject:	Subscribe

E-Mail Address:
First Name:
Last Name:

ABOUT THE AUTHOR

New York Times Bestseller author Denise Swanson was a practicing school psychologist for twenty-two years. Fly Me to the Tomb continues Denise Swanson's Deveraux's Dime Store mystery series. She also writes the Scumble River and Chef-to-Go mysteries, and the Change of Heart and Delicious contemporary romance series.

Denise's books have been finalists for the Agatha, Mary Higgins Clark, RT Magazine's Career Achievement, and Daphne du Maurier Awards. She has won the Reviewers Choice Award and was a BookSense 76 Top Pick.

Denise Swanson lives in Illinois with her husband, classical composer David Stybr.

For more information, please check her website http://www.DeniseSwanson.com or find Denise on Facebook at http://www.facebook.com/DeniseSwansonAuthor or follow her on Twitter at DeniseSwansonAu

Printed in Great Britain
by Amazon

23345761R00165